BEAUTIFUL CHAOS

D0631881

The Doctor Who *50th Anniversary Collection*

BEAUTIFUL
CHAOS

GARY RUSSELL

BOOKS

1 3 5 7 9 10 8 6 4 2

First published in 2008 by BBC Books
This edition published in 2013 by BBC Books, an imprint of Ebury Publishing.
A Random House Group Company

Doctor Who is a BBC Wales production for BBC One.
Executive producers: Steven Moffat and Caroline Skinner

The Random House Group Limited Reg. No. 954009
Addresses for companies within the Random House Group can be found at
www.randomhouse.co.uk

A CIP catalogue record for this book is available from the British Library.

ISBN 978 1 849 90518 3

Editorial director: Albert DePetrillo
Editorial manager: Nicholas Payne
Series consultant: Justin Richards
Project editor: Steve Tribe
Cover design: Two Associates © Woodlands Books Ltd, 2012
Production: Alex Goddard

Printed and bound in the USA

To buy books by your favourite authors and register for offers,
visit www.randomhouse.co.uk

INTRODUCTION

Memory is a funny thing – it sums up everything we are, everything we were and everything we'll probably be, because it shapes everything we do. I have long been obsessed with memory, and the loss of it and the effect that has on identity. It's been a running theme in a number of my *Doctor Who* novels over the years. But *Beautiful Chaos* was the first book where I wanted to take it out of sci-fi/fantasy and make it real. And dip a toe into the water of Alzheimer's and the effect it can have on people horribly afflicted with it and those that love them. And the family Noble gave me the perfect opportunity.

But let's take a step back – let's look at the world of *Doctor Who* in 2008 when I wrote this.

David Tennant was the Tenth Doctor. I'd known David for a few years, long before he became the Doctor – he was an actor I had admired ever since I saw him in a special episode of *The Bill*, the Thames TV cop drama, in which he played a psycho who had tied up a girl in the back of a soon-to-be-airless van. He kept his cool as he was interrogated, he played the policemen for fools, he led them down blind alleys and manipulated them while staying so super cool and innocent. Until he was exposed and the girl saved. And then in an absolute tour de force of TV acting, he tore the final scene up, metaphorically and literally as his character's insanity exploded, shocking the policemen and the viewers with its ferocity and believability and vulnerability too. I knew then he was an actor to watch. I sought him out and directed him a couple of times (he's played nasty Nazis, emotional Scotsmen and sadistic soldiers for me). Then he went to do *Casanova* on telly for Russell T Davies and Julie Gardner. Who then made him the Doctor. Cos they're smart like that.

So I knew what he was capable of as the Doctor and, by 2008, I'd had a chance to see that close up, not just on TV but in studio, at readthrough sessions, etc., because I was working on the show by then. And I wanted to capture that energy, that slightly manic unpredictability but above all, that amazing intellect, in words, for this book. I wanted a book that reflected how I saw the Tenth Doctor.

Donna Noble – how I clapped when I heard she was to be played Catherine Tate. Inspired casting and, like all good comic actors, sixty times more talented than many gave her credit for beforehand. Seriously, you don't get to do all that stuff in her sketch shows without being a brilliant actress – long before you become the best comedienne. I remember watching her at a readthrough for *Planet of the Ood* (I read in the Oods – she thanked me afterwards and I was smitten) - the way she could turn Donna on a penny, one minute all in-yer-face sarcasm, the next, the most astonishingly emotional gut-wrenching torment. I wasn't the only one with damp eyes as she read through that sequence where she hears the Oodsong in the cells. Again, I knew I had to capture that in print – the loud-mouthed aggression that covered this most emotional and sensitive character always fighting to get out.

Both the Doctor and Donna were a testament to Russell's writing and creativity, and they always felt utterly real and normal to me. Stripping away the fake eccentricity that often plagued the Doctor in the classic series and replacing that with heart and soul worked wonders for this fan.

But then there's Wilfred Mott. Wilf. Gramps. (Once known as Sid the Newspaper Seller.) Along with Sylvia, Donna's mum played so beautifully understatedly by Jacqueline King, Bernard Cribbins took that great cliché of the slightly fuddy-duddy granddad and made him shine, made him so utterly gorgeous you wanted him to be your granddad. Isn't that the best thing that can come out of good television writing and good television acting? You wish someone was your granddad, because you love them so much, so quickly?

Into this, I brought in my own character – Nettie, Wilf's would-be 'girlfriend' who gives as good as she gets, utterly aware of where she fits into the family dynamic (Donna adores her, Sylvia sees her as a threat) but never oversteps her boundaries. (Russell even gave her a mention in *The End of Time Part One* – you have no idea how cool that feels!!) Everything should be perfect for her and Wilf – if it wasn't for the Alzheimer's that will, she and Wilf know, eventually destroy her. No one knows when, but they know it will in time. And that's the tragic thing – amidst alien invasions, mad computers, a couple of sparky kids and the delightfully spunky Miss Oladini, Nettie and Wilf are Romeo and Juliet, Calvin and Hobbes, and Eric and Hattie all rolled into one.

At least – that's what I intended. I have no way of knowing if it worked for the reader – I can only hope it did. All I've said is that these were my intentions – to write a story about loss, sadness, triumph and living the only life we have, despite – or even because of – what fate hands us.

All I know is I made Russell T Davies cry (so he says; he was probably being nice), and I had the biggest compliment of my life ever from Bernard Cribbins, who read the audio abridgement on CD. 'You wrote that? I thought because the author's name included Russell, it was him under a false name. Because it was so emotional and heart-breaking.' I didn't know what to say to that (I suspect he was also just being nice) because, although *Beautiful Chaos* is, in my eyes at least, the single best thing I've ever written, I'm well aware there's a hundred better *Doctor Who* novels out there written by far more accomplished and talented writers.

I just wanted to write a story about real people coping with real situations against a background of a fantasy adventure story. I learned to *want* to do that from working with Russell for all those years.

I can never thank him enough for giving me the opportunity to do so. But I'll keep on trying...

Gary Russell
August 2012

For Russell and Julie,
for letting me play in the sandbox…

ONE DAY...

It was raining up on the hill, the steady patter-patter-patter hitting the vast golfing umbrella like bullets on tin. Truth be told, it was raining everywhere, but up on the hill, here in the allotment, that was the only place Wilfred Mott really cared about it raining right now.

Whenever it rained, he couldn't help but remember. That awful, awful day when *he* had come to the house, bringing Donna with him. Unconscious, unable to remember anything. For her own safety.

Wilf remembered that final sight of the Doctor, soaked in the rain, his face streaked with water, hair drooping, clothes clinging tight to his skinny body. And his eyes, his eyes looked so haunted, so sad, so lost. So, so old. They looked like the eyes of an old man, trapped in a ridiculously young body. So miserable. So alone. So lonely.

Then that marvellous blue box had vanished as Wilf saluted it.

And he'd never seen the Doctor again.

But that didn't stop him looking, up there. Up into the night sky, up into the stars that were only still there because of Donna. Up at the stars that warmed and illuminated countless planets, with countless lives that owed their continued existence to Donna Noble. Who would never know – who *could* never know. Because if she did…

He didn't want to think about that. He didn't entirely understand it; he just trusted the Doctor. With his life. And the Doctor deserved that trust because he had saved them all.

From the spaceships in the sky, from the Christmas star, from that huge great *Titanic*, from the Adipose, the Sontarans and the Daleks.

And those were just the ones he knew about. He knew from Donna, Donna as she had been before, that there were countless more.

He shook his head at the scale of it all. And how small and insignificant he was in comparison. But he didn't really mind about that. Because the honour had been in knowing the Doctor.

He reached into a damp pocket and pulled out an old leather wallet. And from inside that, he pulled out some photographs.

One showed Donna on her wedding day, the wedding that had never happened. Donna believed she had never even made it to the altar because poor Lance had got caught up in that business with the Christmas Star attacking the streets of London. Lance had died then – that was the story he'd told her. Indeed, it was the story Wilf told everyone. And he also told Donna that she had been so traumatised by Lance's death, that she'd gone to Egypt to get over the shock.

Whatever it was that the Doctor had done to her

memories made her brain accept the story and find a way to fit it together so she was convinced that was indeed what had happened. Perhaps that was the one good thing that had come out of the 'accident' – her brain did that to cope so, rather than a year or so of blankness, if you put an idea to her, she was able to rationalise it without question. Like a jigsaw where any pieces that didn't fit just reshaped their edges to make sure they did, and formed a slightly different picture but one Donna would never query.

Another picture was of Donna with her mum and dad at her dad's birthday dinner in town. His last birthday as it turned out.

The final photo was of an older woman in a wicker chair, glass of stout in hand, toasting the photographer.

He sighed. So much sadness in the Noble house over the last couple of years.

He put the photos away and took another look through his telescope.

Nothing to see.

'How's the night sky?' asked a voice from behind.

'Hullo, sweetheart,' Wilf said, indicating the newcomer should join him under the umbrella. 'What are you doing here? You'll catch your death.'

'Oh, I'm all right, Dad,' said Sylvia Noble, passing a thermos flask to him. 'Brought you some tea and a bar of chocolate.'

Wilf gratefully took the flask, and they sat in silence for a while, letting the rain create a symphony above them. Then he unscrewed the thermos and offered it to his daughter. She shook her head.

'Donna used to do this,' he muttered.

Sylvia nodded. 'I know. Maybe I need to jog her memory, and she'll start again.'

Wilf shrugged sadly. 'Best not to, eh? Just in case.'

Sylvia changed the subject. 'No blue boxes in the sky tonight then?'

'Not today. But one day I'll see him.'

There was a pause. 'Does it really matter? After all he did to us?'

'Yes, love, it does,' Wilf said. 'I need to know he's out there, still watching over us. Watching over the universe. Because then I know that what Donna has suffered was worth it. Because without him, we're not safe.'

'That's a lot of faith to put in one man, Dad,' Sylvia said quietly. 'And a lot of responsibility.'

Wilf knew that Sylvia didn't like the Doctor, and not just because of what had happened to Donna. She felt that if the Doctor had never come to Earth maybe those Dalek things wouldn't have either. It was an old argument, and the two of them would never agree about it. As a result, they tried not to talk about the Doctor too often.

'He's out there, love. Protecting us. And the Martians. And the Venusians. And God knows who else.' He took a swig of tea. 'You should probably get back in the warm, shouldn't you?'

Sylvia nodded and stood up. 'You going to be much longer?'

'Nah, just want to stay here till eleven, then I'll head back.'

'Donna suggested a drive out to Netty's tomorrow.'

Wilf put his tea down. 'No thanks,' he said quickly.

'Dad, you have to see her some time.' Sylvia reached out and squeezed his hand. 'For your sake if not hers.'

'You shouldn't let Donna go,' Wilf said. 'It's not safe. What if she says something about the Doctor?'

'That's not likely. Even if she does, Donna won't understand and Netty won't be able to explain it.' Sylvia stood up and walked back into the rain. Then she looked back at her old dad. 'We've gone through more heartache than anyone should have to, Dad,' she said quietly. 'Let's not bring any more on ourselves. Please come.'

'I'll think about it. Now go on, before you get a cold.'

Sylvia pointed up to the sky. 'The Doctor would want you to,' she said.

Wilf turned to her with a frown. 'That's beneath you, sweetheart. Please don't.'

Sylvia nodded. 'I'm sorry, Dad.' And she walked back out of the allotments and down the hill.

Wilf watched her receding form until she was out of his view, then unwrapped his chocolate and bit a chunk out of it. He turned for another look through the telescope, cross because Sylvia had invoked the Doctor. Cross because it was a cheap shot. And cross because Sylvia was dead right.

A tear rolled down Wilf's worn cheek.

For so many reasons.

One month after the skies had burned…

FRIDAY

Terry Lockworth checked his mobile, but there was still no signal. Maria was going to be so fed up with him – he'd had to work late but couldn't let her know. No doubt the spag bol would be in the bin tonight. Again. Poor Maria – it wasn't her fault she got fed up with him, but what was he supposed to do. They'd been married three months, had a child on the way (please let it be a girl), and money was tight.

Sure, her dad had given them a deposit for the flat in Boston Manor, but there was still the mortgage, the bills, pre-natal classes, food…

Terry shook his head as he pocketed the phone. Stop moaning, he told himself, and get on with the job, then he'd be home in an hour with any luck. More importantly, he'd be out of this mobile phone black spot in half that, so he could at least phone her then.

He picked up his toolbox and took out the wire-cutters, clipped the plastic coating from the copper wiring and cut the wires. He then yanked the old cables from the junction box and pulled a long thin coil of fibre optics out of the toolbox. These were interesting fibre optics (well, OK, only Terry found them interesting) because they were even finer than normal. A new system, developed by the Americans (aren't they always), and this building was the first in the UK to utilise them. They'd sent Terry on a course in New York six months back to learn about the system. That'd been fun – lots of nights on the town with Johnnie Bates, discovering that it really was the city that never slept. Frequently they'd only just made it to the training classes the next day, hung over but happy.

Terry was sensible enough to know when to party and when to really knuckle down and get the job done, though, and he and Johnnie had come back to England, certified to work on installing these new fibre optics, which made them both popular with their boss and earned them a bit of a bonus.

They'd been promised another bonus if they got this job done and, frankly, it was money in the bank the way they were going. The cabling was easy, it was the removal of the old copper stuff that was taking the time.

Johnnie was a couple of floors above him, closer to the demonstration suite. They'd flipped a coin to see who hung around with the bigwigs and had the chance to nick a cup of tea off the secretaries and PAs and who got the back stairways and service corridors. Terry had lost, of course. No tea for him.

He pulled a screwdriver out of his tool belt and started to open the last junction box, whistling something he'd heard on the radio on the drive over. Anything to pass the time.

If he'd glanced back over the work he'd just done, he

might've been surprised to notice that the fibre-optic cables he'd wired into the previous junction boxes were glowing strangely.

Cables that weren't actually connected to power sources rarely glowed. Never, to be frank. It just didn't happen. Why would it? How could it?

But it was happening: tiny purple pulses of energy, briefly flickering up and down the cabling. Almost like blood pumping through the veins of a huge electronic creature.

Terry didn't notice it because he was looking forwards, looking to see where he was going next, not where he had been.

Which was unfortunate. Not just for Terry Lockworth, whose spaghetti bolognese would indeed go uneaten that night, but also for pretty much the whole human race.

Terry laced the last bit of fibre-optic cabling into the final junction box and screwed it shut for the final time, smiling to himself. Upstairs, Johnnie ought to be receiving proof that the cabling was finished, and his monitors would be telling him that everything was good to go.

As Terry finished tightening up the last screw, a massive bolt of purple alien energy rushed through his screwdriver, his hand, his whole body. It moved so fast that, by the time the miniscule charred flakes that were all that remained of Terry fell to the ground, the screwdriver was only starting to fall away from the screw head.

Of course, Terry was lucky. By dying so suddenly

and violently and efficiently, he was spared what was to come in the next few days.

But he probably wouldn't have seen it quite like that.

Upstairs, in the penthouse suite, Johnnie Bates was linking all the computers into the main admin server of the Oracle Hotel, shining beacon of the architectural brilliance that was the Western Business District Development, commonly known as the Golden Mile, just on the left-hand side of the M4 motorway out of London.

But to the man who owned the hotel, Johnnie was just a little man in grey overalls doing something with wires.

Dara Morgan had, according to the biographies he carefully maintained on his company websites, made his first million in Derry when he was just 26, by creating a popular music torrent site that enabled cheap downloads at six times traditional speeds and with four times traditional MP3 quality.

The music industry loved him. The punters loved him. The government loved him. His mum loved him (well, he assumed she did; they didn't talk so much these days, what with her being kept in a silver urn on the mantelpiece next to his dad).

And the business world loved him. Four years later, and MorganTech was the funding behind the new WBDD, bringing work and development to Hounslow, Osterley and all those other areas of London between Brentford and Heathrow Airport that he'd never heard of prior to buying up the land.

With a personal portfolio of around £65m, he was one step away from being a megastar, already wining and dining with the Trumps, Gateses, de Rothschilds, Gettys and half a dozen more movers and shakers with unpronounceable names from around the world. Actually, the names weren't unpronounceable, but Dara Morgan couldn't be bothered to remember them. They just didn't matter to him enough.

What mattered to him right now was getting the suites of his new hotel ready for the demonstration of his new handheld computer. And the little man in the grimy grey overalls was not going quite fast enough.

'Cait?' He clicked his fingers and a power-dressed redhead with thin metal specs and insanely high heels sauntered over.

'Mr Morgan, sir?'

Dara Morgan pointed towards the grey overalls man. 'How much longer?' he asked, his soft Northern Irish accent unusually snappy.

Caitlin nodded her understanding and strode over to ask the man for information.

Dara Morgan smiled inwardly, watching Caitlin move. He appreciated her on so many levels, but her beauty was pretty high on the list.

Everyone in his organisation was from Derry or surrounding districts of Northern Ireland. More importantly, they were all people he'd grown up with. All hearing stories from parents and older siblings about the strife, the killings, the honour. The marches, the troops, the recriminations and punishment beatings.

It was history to Dara Morgan, something from

another age, almost. His generation had no time to care about the Struggles, any more than they cared about supposed potato famines or Oliver Cromwell. That was ancient history. Dara Morgan and MorganTech were the future. In so many ways.

He ran a hand through his shoulder-length hair and then took out his mobile, pausing to smell the scent of shampoo on his fingers.

It was so important to be clean. To look nice and smell better.

At school, they'd diagnosed it as a form of OCD, as if an obsessive compulsion to wash his hands any time he came into contact with another person was something bad! People carried germs and, while he didn't think for one moment he was going to be struck down with malaria just by shaking hands with a stranger, it wasn't unreasonable to groom oneself every so often.

School never understood him, he recalled vaguely. It was too small, probably too focused on curriculums and timetables and sports.

He couldn't wait to leave, and had done so the moment he'd finished his exams. No sixth form, college or university for him. Straight into business, straight into IT, the future of the world, straight into creating an MP3 system for the troglodytes who thought *Big Brother* and *The X-Factor* were the be all and end all of television culture. He'd needed them, of course, because they'd helped him reach his potential – they'd been the first rungs on the ladder to success. To ruling the world, through business. He had no desire to actually rule the world, it was full of too many thick people fighting over oil and territory and God to be a sensible plan to run it. But he could dominate in technology, see off the current so-called giants and buy access into the homes and workplaces of everyone on the planet.

That was enough.

And at tomorrow's press demonstration, that plan would be taking its first step.

Caitlin returned and said the man was waiting on a call from another man in some service area on the mezzanine floor and he'd be done.

Dara Morgan glanced over – the overalled man was trying to call.

'Tell your friend,' Dara Morgan said to Caitlin, 'that he won't get through to his colleague. The service areas are blocked to cellular signals. Tell him to use a terminal. If the fibre optics are connected, it'll link straight to his associate's mobile.'

Caitlin nodded and passed the message on.

Dara Morgan watched as the overalled man inserted the fibre-optic connection into the back of his laptop and dialled via that.

There was a flash of purple and, where the workman had been kneeling, there was now just a pile of ashes. A burnt, acrid smell wafted over, and Dara Morgan wrinkled his nose in distaste. Burned flesh, melted fabric and sweat. Vile.

'Well,' said Caitlin, 'that bodes well, sir.'

Dara Morgan clapped his hands loudly, and everyone else in the room, all of whom had ignored the death of Johnnie Bates, turned to face him.

'People, it would appear the hotel is wired. Or "fibred", I should say.'

There was a polite ripple of laughter.

'Tomorrow, we take over the world.'

'Oi!'

A word/phrase/guttural noise, spluttered with a splash of indignation, a twist of sarcasm and a great gulp of volume.

No matter how hard he tried, the Doctor couldn't help but sigh every time he heard it. Usually because the indignation, sarcasm and especially the volume were all aimed in his direction.

He sighed and turned back to face Donna Noble, Queen of the 'Oi's.

And she wasn't there.

Just the TARDIS, parked between two council dumpsters. Quite neatly, if he said so himself.

Oh.

Ah.

Right.

'Sorry,' he said to the TARDIS door, then walked back and unlocked it, revealing Donna stood on the threshold. 'I assumed you were already outside.'

'Which bit of "I'm right behind you" didn't quite make sense, then?' Donna asked oh-so-politely, with a characteristic head wobble that actually meant she wasn't feeling all that polite at all. 'Which bit of "wait for me" bypassed your hearing? Which section of "I'm just putting on something nice" vanished into the ether?'

There was no way for the Doctor to worm out of that

one. So he just shrugged. 'I said I was sorry.'

'"Sorry"?'

'Yeah, "sorry". What else do you want?'

'Are you "sorry" that you didn't hear me? "Sorry" that you locked me inside your alien spaceship? Or "sorry" that you hadn't even noticed I wasn't with you?'

Each time, Donna pinged the word 'sorry' so it sounded like the least apologetic word in the English language and took on a whole new meaning that linguists could argue over the exact implication of for the next twelve centuries.

'No way I can win this,' the Doctor said, 'so I'm just gonna let it go, all right?'

Donna opened her mouth to speak again, but the Doctor reached forward and put a finger on her lips. 'Hush,' he said.

Donna hushed.

And winked.

'I win!'

And then she gave him that fantastic, amazing grin that she always did when she was teasing him – and he gave her that sigh that admitted he'd been caught out yet again.

It was a game. A game that two friends who'd gone through so much together played instinctively with one another.

Familiarity, friendship and fun. The three Fs that summed up the time shared by these two adventurers.

She slipped an arm around his and pulled him close. 'So, what's the skinny, Skinny?'

The Doctor nodded towards Chiswick High Road

and the hustle and bustle of the traffic, and quickly dragged her out onto the main street, ready to get lost in the crowds.

Except there weren't any. Indeed, there weren't really very many people around at all, just a couple of kids on a skateboard on the opposite pavement and an old man walking his dog.

The Doctor raised his other hand. 'Not raining,' he said.

'Well spotted, Sherlock,' said Donna. 'Sunday?'

'You wanted Friday the fifteenth of May 2009, Donna. That's what I set the TARDIS for.'

Donna laughed. 'In which case it's probably a Sunday in August 1972.'

The Doctor poked his head into a newsagents, smiling at the man behind the counter, who was listening to his MP3 player and ignoring his potential customer completely.

The Doctor looked at the nearest newspaper. 'Friday 15th May 2009,' he confirmed to Donna.

'So where is everyone?'

'Maybe it's lunchtime,' the Doctor suggested. 'Or maybe Chiswick's no longer the hub of society it was a month ago. Shall we walk to your place?'

'You're coming?'

The Doctor looked as though the thought of not going with Donna hadn't crossed his mind. 'Oh. Umm. Well, I was going to.'

'Doctor, why are we here?'

'It's the first anniversary of your father's death.'

'And, grateful as I'm sure she is for you saving the

world from the Sontarans, I'm not quite sure my mum's gonna be overjoyed to see you, today of all days.'

'Your granddad will.'

'Yeah? Good, take him out for a pint tonight in the Shepherd's Hut, but to start with I want to see them on my own.' Donna was still holding his hand, and she squeezed it gently. 'You understand, don't you?'

He smiled. 'Course I do. Wasn't thinking. Sorry.'

'Let's not start that up again, yeah?' Donna let go of his hand. 'I'm gonna get some flowers and walk home. Why don't I meet you back here, this time, tomorrow?'

'Here. Tomorrow. Sold.' The Doctor winked at her and started walking off. 'Nice flower shop on the corner thataway,' he called out. 'Ask for Loretta and say I sent you.'

He turned a corner and was gone.

Donna took a breath and walked in the direction he'd pointed.

A year ago. Today.

Adipose. Pyroviles. Oods with brains in their hands. Even Sontaran probic vents, Hath and talking skeletons all seemed simple in comparison to what was going to happen this afternoon.

Because this afternoon Donna had to go back and be there for her mum and probably relive not just last year, but the days and weeks that had followed, funerals, telling people, memorials, notices in papers, sorting out the financial side of things, finding the will... None of it had been easy on Donna's mum. Hadn't been that easy on Donna, truth be told, and a year ago that would have been her overriding thought. Donna Noble, putting herself first. But not now – just a short time with the Doctor had shown her that she wasn't the woman she had been then.

And Granddad, poor Granddad, bringing back memories of Nan's passing, he'd bravely soldiered on for everyone else's sake, trying to sort out solicitors and funeral directors and suchlike.

Not that Mum had been weak or feeble – Sylvia Noble wasn't like that, and they'd been prepared for Dad's death, well, as much as you can be, but it still haunted her. She could see it in her mum's eyes, it was like someone had cut an arm and a leg off, and Mum just coped as best she could. Thirty-eight years they'd been married.

Donna sighed. 'Miss you, Dad,' she said out loud as she came to a halt outside a laundrette called Loretta's.

Her phone buzzed with a text message, and she read it.

UMMM. ACTUALLY MIGHT BE WRONG. LORETTA'S MIGHT NOT BE FLORIST. SORRY.

How did he do that? He didn't even have a mobile as far as Donna knew. That sonic screwdriver perhaps? Was there nothing it couldn't do?

Shoving the phone back into her coat pocket, Donna decided she'd be better off heading towards Turnham Green. She knew there was a florist there.

Men. Alien men. Useless, the lot of them.

Lukas Carnes hated technology. Which made him a bit weird, according to all his mates. His mum had a PC, but Lukas avoided using it if possible, other than to type up school essays once he'd done them in longhand. He had an MP3 player which his younger brother (who was eight) had to actually put music onto for him. And don't even get him started on the problems associated with using a DVD-R.

He was, he'd decided on his fifteenth birthday, a throwback to an earlier time, when technically savvy guys were called geeks and girls ran a mile from them. Sadly for Lukas, most girls he knew wanted a bloke who could download music at twenty paces and unlock a mobile that had come from a dodgy stall in Shepherds Bush Market.

So Lukas didn't have a girlfriend.

Which just added fuel to his passionate loathing for tech. He accepted that he needed it, he just didn't want to understand it. His brain wasn't wired to understand MP3 compressions and 3G and GPS tracking systems. He just wanted to press an ON button and have it all work. Wasn't that what his mum's age group had gone through all that First/Second/Third Generation stuff for? So that he could press buttons and things worked without being out of date in six months and redundant in twelve. On TV they talked about the days when you could click your fingers and doors would open, when you could walk into a room and say 'lights' and a computer would turn everything on, just to the right level.

God. He was his grandmother! Next thing, he'd be saying he couldn't understand pop music and what sex was that person on *Popworld*?

Fifteen, not fifty, Lukas.

So why was he standing in the local branch of Discount Electronics, watching a demonstration of the newest Fourth Generation Processor on some laptop thinner than a piece of cardboard?

Because his brother, his 8-year-old, technically savvy, brother Joe had asked him. Well, strictly speaking, Mum had asked him. With Joe's dad gone, just like Lukas's before him, the older boy had become de facto father to his little brother. Which suited Lukas, cos secretly he adored Joe, not that he'd ever tell him that. And cos little brothers needed to know who was boss, and Lukas's power would be lost at the first sign of weakness.

And Joe had acted up really badly after his dad went, getting into trouble at school and on the estate, and Mum had been visited by the police twice.

So Lukas had taken Joe aside and explained as best he could to an 8-year-old that it wasn't Mum's fault his dad had gone, nor was it Joe's, and messing about with the older kids, helping them nick cars and stuff wasn't helping Mum.

After a few months, Joe had calmed down. But now he hung on to Lukas at all times, and kicked off if his big brother didn't take him everywhere. Lukas had even started taking Joe to junior school before heading off to Park Vale High. Which Mum appreciated no end, so that was good.

But occasionally, Lukas wanted to kick off by himself, be alone, not be the responsible one.

Today was a day like that, but here he was with Joe, watching this new demo along with thirty other people, all tucked into a shop that probably safely took ten people at most. God help them if there was a fire.

A large (in every direction) woman moved in front of them, so Lukas hoisted Joe up into his arms so he could see better. This meant Lukas could see nothing. So while Joe (how heavy was he getting?) watched intently, Lukas's gaze drifted round the shop.

A skinny guy in a blue suit was tapping away at a demonstration laptop that was probably going to be out of date by the end of today. The guy was searching for something on the internet – Lukas could see repeated screens showing a search engine (ooh, technical term!) – and frowning. He clearly wasn't getting the results he wanted.

The man reached into his pocket and took out a shiny tube, like a marker pen, and pointed it at the screen. At first, Lukas thought he was going to write on the laptop's screen but instead the end of the pen glowed blue, and Lukas watched in amazement as the images on the screen downloaded and changed at a phenomenal rate. No, an impossible rate. The blue-suited man took a pair of thick black glasses out of another pocket and put them on as he stared intently at the changing screens. Surely he couldn't read that fast?

He became aware that Lukas was watching him and smiled, almost sheepishly. The shiny pen went back into a pocket, the glasses into another.

Lukas realised his mouth was open, so he snapped it shut.

Blue Suit Guy winked at Lukas and was about to leave the shop, when he reached forward and picked up a leaflet about the demonstration Lukas's little brother was watching. And then he looked at the crowd and wandered over.

Lukas quickly switched his attention back to the demo. Or at least to the back of Fat Lady's head.

After a few minutes of listening to some blonde droning on about how revolutionary the new computer system was, Blue Suit Guy shrugged and muttered about 'impossible' and 'not on this planet' and 'contradicting the Shadow Proclamation's Eighteenth Protocol', at which point Lukas decided that, shiny pen-thing or not, this guy was probably a nutter. Maybe he should get Joe away from him, just in case the guy had a knife.

Lukas leaned forward to whisper in Joe's ear that maybe it was time to go home, when Blue Suit Guy nudged him.

'So, everyone's inside all the electronics shops, yeah?'

'Sorry?'

'The streets were pretty empty. As I walked along, I realised everyone was in shops like this, watching these demos.'

'Today's the launch,' Lukas found himself explaining. 'Everyone's interested.'

'You're not,' Blue Suit Guy replied.

Lukas shrugged. 'Kid brother is.'

'Ah. I see.'

Lukas tried to step away, but was hemmed in by another man on one side and Fat Lady in front.

Blue Suit Guy got his shiny pen out again. 'Don't mind me,' he said.

But Lukas did mind him. A lot.

'Why are you here?' he asked.

Blue Suit Guy shrugged. 'Well, firstly, I'm letting a friend go home for a bit. Secondly, I was wondering why everyone was in here. And fourthly, I'm now really concerned by the technology in that laptop.'

Lukas knew he'd regret this. 'And thirdly?'

'Thirdly?' Blue Suit Guy looked confused, and then grinned as if something had popped back into his head. 'Oh yes, thirdly, I came looking for you, Lukas Samuel Carnes.' He held out a hand. 'I'm the Doctor and I'm here to save your life.'

Dara Morgan sipped his coffee slowly. Partly because it showed he had good manners, and partly because it was too hot to do anything else. But it probably looked like good manners to Mr Murakami and his delegation.

'So, Mr Morgan,' the Japanese banker was saying, 'do we have a deal?'

Dara Morgan's blue eyes twinkled mischievously as he glanced over at Caitlin, standing by the office door. 'What do you think, Cait?'

Caitlin walked over, her long legs and short skirt clearly drawing the eye of some of Mr Murakami's entourage but not, Dara Morgan observed, Mr Murakami himself.

Good.

'I think it's a good deal, sir,' she purred. 'If Murakami-San can get the M-TEK out throughout the East by Sunday, it will be… superb.'

Dara Morgan flicked his hair out of his eyes. 'Just under two days, 3.30pm Tokyo time. Doable?'

Mr Murakami frowned. 'Why Sunday? It's ludicrously short notice.'

Dara Morgan just smiled. 'Let's just say, it's what the entire deal hinges on. I need that guarantee, Murakami-San, or I go elsewhere.'

'But that way, you have even less chance of a deal to be in place by then,' the Japanese man said.

Dara Morgan nodded at this. 'I know. But let's face it, with the money that the M-TEK will make, smaller companies than yours, hungrier ones perhaps, will go that extra mile to meet my... MorganTech's requirements.' He sipped his coffee again. 'It'll be in the contract, with penalty clauses.'

'Which will be?'

'Catastrophic. For the whole of Japan.'

Mr Murakami's people moved an inch closer to their man. 'Was that a threat, Mr Morgan?' he asked softly.

'No,' said Dara Morgan. 'I don't do threats. Barbarians do threats. Idiots do threats. I just state facts.'

'It is a great opportunity,' Caitlin cut in. 'Please, think about it over dinner. Tonight. At our expense.'

'Alas, we cannot join you,' Dara Morgan added, 'but you are at liberty to pick any restaurant in London that takes your fancy and all expenses will be covered by MorganTech. Indeed I insist.'

'All expenses?'

'Relating to food and drink, yes.'

'Ah. In that case, you shall have my answer by midnight tonight.' Mr Murakami stood and Dara Morgan did the same, giving a slight bow as he did so. Mr Murakami responded likewise, including Caitlin in the deference, and she nodded to him and the others in his party.

Formalities over, the Japanese delegation headed for the door of the suite, but Mr Murakami turned back one last time. 'Seriously, why Sunday? Why 3.30 in the afternoon?'

'Because something big is happening all over the globe on Monday at 3pm UK time. That's 11pm Tokyo time. But we all need deals in place. I too have made a deal, you see, but it's rather like a chain in a property purchase: one link breaks and the whole deal comes tumbling down. Then we all suffer.'

'All?'

'Universally.' Dara Morgan threw a sideways glance at Caitlin, and she immediately moved to escort Mr Murakami out of the room.

A moment later, the Japanese were gone and Caitlin was back at Dara Morgan's side. He was standing at a massive picture window, a huge panoramic view over West London. He could see the new Wembley Stadium, Centrepoint, the London Eye and other tall London structures.

'Monday,' he smiled, 'and this planet is Madam Delphi's.'

Caitlin nodded. 'At last. Revenge is hers.'

They took each other's hands and held on tightly, and looked to the computer screens, which appeared to be humming a tune, ever so slightly, causing waveforms on one of the screens to pulsate fractionally in time.

'Welcome back,' they said to her, together.

Donna stood at the end of Brookside Road and took a deep breath. It hadn't been that long since she'd been here last (indeed, for her mum, it was probably slightly less time), but every time she 'came home' there were awkward moments. 'Where have you been?' and 'Are you still hanging around with that awful Doctor person?' and 'Why don't you call?' and 'Have you got a job yet?'

Of course, Granddad Wilf knew where she was, she'd told him everything right from the off. But her mum, well, she wasn't someone who'd understand. Wasn't someone who'd think saving Oods, stopping generational wars or ensuring Charlemagne met the Pope actually equated with a 'good' job typing up notes or placing stationery orders.

Taking a deep breath, she walked towards the house that hadn't actually been her home for too long.

After her disastrous wedding and slightly less disastrous trip to Egypt, her parents had moved from their terraced house where Donna had grown up into this new semi. It had been an upheaval, compounded as it was by Donna not having a job and Wilf originally being cross because he thought he'd have to leave his astronomer buddies behind. As it turned out, of course, the allotments were easier to get to from the new house, so he was happy after all.

But Donna's dad hadn't been well for a long time, and in many ways the move had been his idea, his desire to find somewhere new to be, to give him a bit of challenge. He'd got bored in the old house. He'd built all the cupboards, shelved all the walls, painted all the ceilings he was ever able to do, and he needed something new to keep him active since his illness had made him take early retirement. Doing up the new place to Mum's quite stringent specifications would be exactly the right challenge.

They had been there three months before Dad passed. Donna and Wilf had taken on the mantle of doing all those odd jobs Dad had been going to do, but they were never quite right, they were never 'how your dad would have done it'. Which wasn't altogether surprising – Wilf was twenty-odd years older, and Donna had never lifted a paintbrush or hammer in her life before.

God. How shallow was Donna Noble before she met the Doctor again? Before she learned not just to stand on her own two feet but realise that she could. Her family life was a real chicken and egg situation. Had she been useless at home because her parents had always let her be, or did her mum think she was useless because she was?

And talking about it, talking about anything, with Sylvia Noble was rarely a positive experience. Donna would love to say that her mum's bitterness and resentment was because of Dad's death, but the truth was Sylvia had always been disappointed in her daughter. She rarely hid it. And Donna never understood why. Had she wanted a son? Had she wanted a high-flying lawyer or company executive daughter who would be rich enough to send her parents off to live in the country in a little sixteenth-century cottage where they could keep goats? Had it got worse since Dad had died? Would it have been better if she had got married to Lance? Should she have told Mum the truth about that day? Like she had Granddad recently? Probably not, because Sylvia didn't like people being open and honest. 'Those bleeding hearts who wear their hearts on their sleeves' was an analogy she'd tortured once, and it summed up her opinion of people actually being honest.

Donna remembered reading a magazine article once about how parents could never truly hope to understand teenaged offspring and their best bet for harmonious living was just to tolerate those three or four nightmare years. But was there a manual for sons and daughters on how to deal with negative parents? It was impossible to actually argue with a mother – they had an inbuilt 'guilt trip' button to press that forbade you saying all the things you wanted to say to them, whatever they threw at you.

Donna loved her mum, no two ways about that. And she had no doubt that Sylvia Noble loved her daughter.

She just wasn't entirely sure they actually liked each other that much.

'Hullo, Donna,' called Mrs Baldrey from opposite. 'Had a nice trip?'

'Yes thanks,' Donna smiled back. 'How's Seymour?'

'Oh fine. Still complaining about his prostate,' the neighbour groaned.

Donna thought that conversation had gone as far as she wanted it to go, frankly, and speeded up her pace towards home.

A cat sat by a lamppost, warily watching Donna approach, not quite sure if she was friend or foe. Donna made squeaky noises to attract its attention.

It bolted.

Ah well.

Mum's car was outside on the road (you have a drive, Mum, use it) and Donna touched the bonnet as she passed. Cold. Mum hadn't been out today then. Funny how she'd picked up these little things from travelling with the Doctor to find things out. Like whether a car had been driven. The old Donna would never have thought about that. The old Donna wouldn't have cared.

The old Donna was gone.

Thank God – her life was a trillion times better these days.

If only she could involve her mum in it, though. That last little piece of the puzzle, that last bit of acceptance from each of them.

'Oh there you are, Lady,' said a familiar voice from behind her. 'I wondered if we'd see you today.'

Donna didn't bother turning around. 'Hello, Mum,' she said.

'Oh yes, "Hello, Mum" – because that's enough isn't it. One minute the air's choking with exhaust fumes, the next the sky's on fire, and that's it. No idea where my only daughter is. No calls, no texts, not even a message sent to your granddad, so he can shut me up. Nothing.'

Donna stopped in the street and turned to face her mother, automatically tugging two of the four shopping bags from her hand to help.

The old Donna wouldn't have considered that either.

'Nice to see you, too,' Donna said. 'Granddad got the kettle on? I could do with a cuppa, loads to tell you.'

Sylvia Noble shrugged and stomped off ahead of

her daughter. 'You know what today is, don't you,' she called back.

And Donna stopped dead.

Of course she knew what today was. Why the hell did she think she was there? How dare she even ask that question?

The front door opened and Sylvia pushed passed Granddad Wilf and went wordlessly into the kitchen.

'Do you know what she just asked me?' Donna hissed at him after kissing his cheek.

Wilf raised his eyes to heaven. 'It's gonna be one of them days, isn't it?'

Donna opened her mouth to reply, then stopped.

The old Donna would have gone off on one, there and then. The old Donna would've started a row with her mum, throwing around words like 'attitude' and 'whatever' and 'selfish'.

New Donna didn't.

Because new Donna, frustrating as it was, understood that what Sylvia Noble probably wanted and needed today was a good cry.

But being Sylvia 'I don't wear my heart on my sleeve' Noble meant she'd never do that.

And sadly it was going to be new Donna's job today to ensure she did, before bottling it up caused her mum more damage than it already had.

The Doctor was striding down Chiswick High Road, glancing into various shops where people were staring at the new laptop demonstrations. 'It's just a computer,' he muttered. 'Why so much interest?'

'They're already out of date,' said a young voice beside him. 'The M-TEK – that's the future.'

The Doctor looked over, then down. The speaker barely reached knee height. It was a little boy. The Doctor had seen him before somewhere – then running towards him, he saw Lukas Carnes, and realised this was the little brother he'd been carrying.

'Joe!' yelled Lukas. 'How'd you get away from me so fast?'

'I'm not your prisoner,' Joe yelled back, and the Doctor gave the arrived-but-out-of-breath Lukas a look that said 'Oh, that told you, mate'.

Lukas pulled Joe back from the Doctor. 'Leave him alone,' Lukas snapped at him. 'Touch him and I'll have the police here.' As if to underline this, Lukas had his mobile out and ready.

The Doctor didn't bother pointing out that Joe had found *him*. Nor did he point out that Lukas was clearly only being aggressive because of what the Doctor had said in the other shop.

He had to remember that people didn't always like getting hints about their future. Always tripped him up, that one.

Spoilers, someone once said.

'How do you mean you are going to save my life?'

The Doctor shrugged. 'Done it.'

'Done what?'

'Saved your life.'

'How? When and why?'

The Doctor drew his psychic paper out of his inner jacket pocket and showed it to Lukas. It had the right date on it, the name of the shop and the message SAVE LUKAS SAMUEL CARNES'S LIFE BY STOPPING HIS BROTHER BUYING AN M-TEK.

'Dunno who wrote it,' the Doctor said, 'cos I don't recognise the handwriting. But it appeared on the paper about twenty minutes after I arrived in Chiswick. Bad form to ignore messages, I always think. So, you've been saved, my job is done, all I need to do now is find out whether Loretta's is a laundrette, a florist or a coffee shop in this time period. It's one of those in 2009 but I'm not sure which.'

'Laundrette,' said Joe.

Lukas pulled Joe behind him. 'Don't talk to that man,' he scolded his kid brother.

'But you're talking to him,' Joe protested, not unreasonably.

'That's different,' Lukas said, realising with horror that this was exactly what his mum used to say when she'd said something he considered hypocritical or unfair.

The Doctor turned away. 'Nice to meet you, boys, but I thought I might wander off to a lovely restaurant in Brentford, down by the canal there, to pass the time before I meet up with my friend.'

'What?' said Lukas, mentally kicking himself for caring. Just let the weirdo go, he urged himself. But his mouth wouldn't stop asking questions. 'What would've happened if Joe had got an M-TEK?'

And the Doctor looked at him. 'No idea. I don't know what an M-TEK is. I assumed it was that laptop you were thinking of buying. I did a search, but I couldn't find any reference to it. Then I saw you watching the demo, like everyone else appears to be, so I guess that's the M-TEK.'

'No,' said Joe, pushing forwards. 'That's the new Psiryn Book Plus. It's rubbish. I wanted an M-TEK.'

'But I wasn't planning to buy one,' Lukas added. 'For Joe or me.'

'So what's an M-TEK then?' the Doctor frowned.

Lukas sighed. 'How can you save me from it, if you don't know what it is?'

'If I knew everything I was saving people from before I tried saving them, I'd save very few people cos I'd be spending all day researching what I was saving them from, wouldn't I?'

Lukas and Joe glanced at each other.

'You're funny,' said Joe.

'Thank you,' the Doctor said.

Lukas shook his head. 'Home,' he said to Joe. 'Come on.' He all but dragged his little brother away.

'Bye, Doctor,' Joe called back.

The Doctor waved as the two boys vanished into a side street. Then he started to wander towards the lower end of Chiswick, and the M4 flyover, towards Brentford. And that nice Italian in the square. Luna Piena. He hadn't had a decent Italian meal in years. Centuries perhaps.

SINCE 1492 was written on the psychic paper.

Which was weird, because the psychic paper didn't work like that. At least, it hadn't in the past. It was bad enough that people were using it more and more to send him messages these days, but when it started answering him unbidden, it was time perhaps to give it a two-thousand leaf service.

He shoved the leather wallet with the paper in it back inside his jacket pocket and tried to forget all about it.

At the back of his mind, though, he still had a nagging worry, an echo of Lukas Samuel Carnes's not unreasonable question: what was an M-TEK and how had he saved Lukas from it?

To which the answer was obvious.

He hadn't.

So Lukas was still in danger (if the psychic paper was to be trusted), and he had to save him.

Oh, and another question needed an answer.

How had Lukas's little brother Joe known to call him 'Doctor'?

So… Luna Piena or getting embroiled?

It wasn't much of a decision was it? Food was nice, but a mystery, that was far better.

He wondered how Donna was getting on and whether he should stop by and tell her he might be busy for a couple of days.

Nah, she was probably best left alone to do family stuff.

And so he turned around and headed up the side street after the two boys.

On the penthouse suite floor of the Oracle Hotel, Dara Morgan and Caitlin were staring at a bank of flat-screen monitors, connected to the computer, by the fibre-optic cables which Terry Lockworth and Johnnie Bates had died setting up earlier.

On most of the screens was a sine wave, pulsating rhythmically, as if the computer were breathing. Which it was. Sort of.

But on the largest, central screen was an image, a photo, taken from CCTV cameras that had been automatically hacked into and enhanced to almost perfect resolution, according to the parameters the computer had been set to.

'Madam Delphi,' Dara Morgan asked. 'What is this?'

His finger traced the outline. It was a tall blue box standing in a Chiswick alleyway between two dumpsters.

'The TARDIS,' replied a strong, feminine voice, echoing across the room, the sine waves on the other screens pulsating and changing as it spoke.

'He is here,' Caitlin said. 'Already.'

Dara Morgan nodded enthusiastically. 'Five hundred years, as the legends foretold. The Chaos Bringer.'

'Five hundred and seventeen years, one month, four days,' corrected Madam Delphi. 'We did not allow for cosmic shift five hundred years ago. That was a tad… unfortunate.'

Caitlin addressed the computer. 'But Madam Delphi, there have been other attempts…'

'And because of that cosmic shift, because the universe breathes shallow breaths as well as deep ones, the alignments have never been perfect.'

'But on Monday all will be perfect.' Dara Morgan stroked Madam Delphi's surfaces. 'And you will have your revenge.'

'On the Doctor. On mankind. On the entire universe,' Caitlin said excitedly.

'Oh sure,' Madam Delphi pulsed her sine waves.

'Absolutely. Love the revenge thing, my darlings. But especially on the Doctor.'

It was 5pm in the UK. So, in sunny New York, the Big Apple shadows stretched as the midday sun beamed down, covering the city in an unusually humid blanket.

This was not good news for the inhabitants of the MorganTech office block on 52nd and 7th. The air conditioning had failed a few hours earlier, and the automatic drinking fountains had ceased pumping cool water into the water coolers. The main reason for this was that all the power in the block was off. The main doors had failed first, followed by the phones, IT equipment, air-con and so on.

It had taken Melissa Carson on reception a few minutes to twig that everything had gone wrong. She tried calling maintenance. Obviously, as everything maintenance maintained had failed, there was no way to get maintenance to maintain anything. This had annoyed Melissa, so she had committed the corporate crime of leaving her desk to find someone.

Instead, what she found – other than stalled elevators probably containing rapidly dehydrating passengers, and internally locked electronic doors – was a pile of dust on the floor by a junction box in the basement. Presumably maintenance had been doing something to the wiring and had fused the systems. It didn't occur to Melissa (and why should it?) that the ashes she was wiping casually off her Dolce & Gabbana heels had once been a guy she'd waved to earlier that day called Milo. But she did wonder where Milo and the guys were.

Casually, as she stomped back to her desk in frustration, she flicked the open junction box shut.

At once, the newly installed fibre optics came to life, pulsing purple light throughout their network. The occupants of the building, already whingeing about stuck lifts, no air-con and crashed computers, had all of ten seconds to register their PCs flicker back into life. As office workers do, everyone reached forward and touched their keyboards.

A massive arc of purple light pulsated throughout the building, touching everyone, not just those using the PCs. Not a person, a roach or a moth in the basement was spared the purple pulse of energy.

Forty-two seconds after Melissa Carson had shut that junction box, all one hundred and seven humans, eighteen rats, two thousand creatures of various sizes and shapes but with six legs or more and three pigeons on the roof were all dead.

'We have a slight problem, guys,' Madam Delphi pulsed at Dara Morgan and Caitlin. 'The MorganTech building in Manhattan is offline. The terminals are terminal.' There was a noise like an electronic laugh, and the sine waves pulsed accordingly.

Dara Morgan frowned, tapping at another part of Madam Delphi's array of monitors and keyboards.

'I'm not wrong,' the computer reported.

'I know,' Dara Morgan said quickly. 'You're never wrong. I'm trying to ascertain what the problem is.'

'Human error,' Madam Delphi reported. 'What else is it going to be? I mean, let's be honest with each other, you lot are always the weakest links in the chain.'

'We need New York,' Caitlin said.

'Well, we haven't got New York any longer,' said the computer.

'Can you override the pulse?'

'No,' snapped Madam Delphi. 'Too late anyway. Honestly, my sweets, you're wasting your time. I'll see if I can shift resources to a back-up server and start again.'

Dara Morgan lost his cool for the first time in ages. 'Don't you get it? We don't have time to start again. We have to have New York's M-TEKs online at 10am Manhattan time on Monday.'

'It's the city that never sleeps, if I remember my song lyrics,' the computer said.

'Yeah, maybe it never sleeps. But it pretty much stops work at 5pm on a Friday and doesn't go to work at weekends.'

'Oh, my darling boy, have some faith. I've been at this kind of thing across the universe for a few million years now. We'll just have to do a merger this afternoon. A hostile takeover by MorganTech on a small company in… ooh let me guess… oh yes, look, here's one.'

On Madam Delphi's big screen a shot of a smallish (for New York) office building, all chrome and glass with people milling about popped up.

'I'm accessing their systems… now. Ooh yes, lots of people. They do hardware service and repairs, a firm co-owned by the Mafiosa, a Chinese Triad and initially set up by IRA laundering. None of whom know about each other obviously. Easy to take over because none of them are going to stand up and scream about it.'

The image changed to one a little further away. 'Lexington and 3rd, nice spot,' the computer continued. 'I knew a cybercafé there once. It never called back.'

Row after row of figures shot across the screens, too fast for Dara Morgan to even count and then the sine waves returned, pulsing again as Madam Delphi purred at them both.

'Kittel Software Inc, now a subsidiary of MorganTech. I hope you don't mind, I had to agree to allow one Harvey Gellar to remain CEO, with a set of shares and a vote on the board.'

Cait frowned. 'Won't that be a problem?'

'In one hour, eighteen minutes, Mr Gellar will get into the lift... sorry, elevator... and ride it to the ground floor. In one hour, twenty-one minutes, the lift will get stuck between the nineteenth and eighteenth floors. He will press the alarm button. It'll be the last thing he does. They'll find the body within, oh, a couple of hours and assume it was a heart attack. I've already rewritten his terms to ensure that on his death his Irish third cousin, Dara Morgan of MorganTech, inherits everything.'

'I'm not his third cousin...'

'You are now according to FBI files.' Madam Delphi's screens darkened slightly, the sine wave taking on a red hue as it pulsed. 'Your constant underestimation of what I can do, Dara Morgan, is beginning to bore me.'

'I'm sorry.'

'Good. Now then, this new branch of MorganTech will now appear to have been planning to handle Monday's launch of the M-TEK all along. They have the specs, details, customer base, everything. All we need to do is get a couple of flunkies in over the weekend to strip out the wiring and put our fibre optics in. And… there, subcontractors booked and assigned. Easy.'

Caitlin looked at Dara Morgan. 'Yes, Madam Delphi. Easy.'

'Cheers m'dears. Now if it's OK with you kids, I'm just going to download this week's *Coronation Street* omnibus. Whatever will that sweet little David Platt get up to next?'

Sylvia was putting the shopping away in the kitchen. Neatly, everything in its place. Just as always. She was, however, letting the odd drawer or cupboard door slam shut a little noisily.

'What have I done now?' Donna whispered to her granddad from the armchair that faced the TV in the sitting room. Where her dad used to sit and laugh at *The X-Factor*. And repeats of *Dad's Army*. And that programme where… where…

Well, all his programmes, anyway.

And suddenly, she wanted to move to the settee next to her granddad but he moved along it instead, so he was sat close to her armchair.

'Dunno what you mean, darlin',' he said, not catching her eye.

'Right, cos Mum's using IKEA's finest to beat out the drum solo from something Ozzy Osbourne wrote because she's suddenly got an interest in heavy rock, yeah?'

'Oh, she's just…being your mother. You know…'

'No, Granddad. No, I don't know.' Donna sighed and

looked at a local newspaper on the occasional table. Its lead story was about Q-Mart and Betterworth's opening rival supermarkets in Park Vale.

Thrillsville.

'I'm here. Chiswick. London W3. Earth. Yesterday I was on another planet, stopping robots fighting a civil war. A week before that, we were in the Garazone Bazaar riding six-legged horses!' She suddenly grabbed Wilf's hand. 'They had six legs! Six. I mean, how fast were we galloping? It was brilliant. I loved it. And Martian Boy was screaming at the top of his lungs "Where's the off switch?" cos he thought they could be stopped just like that.'

'He's not a Martian though, is he? I thought he said—'

'No, Granddad, he's not a Martian. It's a joke. Remember jokes? You know, that moment when you open your mouth and go ha-ha-ha? We used to do it, even in this house once or twice.'

Donna stared at her granddad's lined face. When did he suddenly get so old? Was that the strain of Dad's passing, too? What happened to that man who used to take her for a spin in his old Aston? Who used to show her off to his old paratrooper mates down at the Social? When did he get replaced by the white-haired old man sitting in front of her?

When did the idea of coming home fill her with such dread? Was this the downside of being with the Doctor? That normality was now alien?

'I got something to tell you, sweetheart,' her granddad said. 'I reckon it'll cheer you up. I hope it does.'

Good news at last. Donna smiled. 'Well, go on then. Spill.'

Her granddad opened his mouth to speak, but Sylvia chose that moment to come into the sitting room and flop onto the settee next to him.

'So, where've you been, Donna Noble?'

Donna opened her mouth to answer, but her granddad got there first. 'She's been horseriding, Sylv. In Dubai.'

'Dubai? How the hell did you afford Dubai?' Sylvia sighed. 'Oh silly me, the Doctor took you, yes?'

Donna nodded. 'Yeah. He paid for it and everything. I nearly married a rich oil sheikh and lived in his harem, but you know what? I thought it was more important to be here today. With you two.'

'Well, that's nice, I'm sure,' Sylvia said. 'Perhaps, if hanging out with the rich and famous of OPEC hasn't been too demanding, you could make us all a cuppa?'

'Course.' Donna stood up but wasn't fast enough to stop Sylvia getting another jibe in. 'Can you remember where the teabags are? And the kettle?'

And that was it. Time to have this out.

'What have I done, Mum? I mean, really, where did it go wrong? All you ever told me was to go out, do things, get a job, live my life. And I do that. And it's still not good enough, is it?' She sat down again. 'I'm still not good enough, am I? Was Dad as disappointed in me as you are?'

'Don't you dare speak about your father like that,' Sylvia yelled, far louder than seemed necessary.

'Now, now—' Wilf started, but Sylvia shushed him

sharply.

'No, no, it's time Lady Muck over there had a few home truths.' Sylvia leaned forward, jabbing at the air with her finger. 'Your grandfather and I are worried sick, you know that? You up and leave with barely a word, you turn up once in a blue moon when it suits you and you're off again. I don't know whether you're alive or dead. I don't know if each time the phone rings it's you telling me you're in Timbuktu, or there's a ring on the doorbell and it'll be the police saying they've found you washed up in the Thames. A letter arrives for you and I put it on the mantelpiece, hoping that somehow that means you'll come home sooner. But after a couple of weeks, I just chuck it on your bed because it doesn't work. It doesn't bring you home. Ever since you met that Doctor bloke, you've become a different person.'

Donna stared at her mum in mute shock. Where had all this come from. 'Why the hell would you assume I'm dead? That's mad.'

'It's not mad, it's not unreasonable. It's what I think. Every day I don't hear from you, I think it more. Maybe if you were a mother, maybe if you'd got kids, stupid, selfish, unthinking kids, you'd understand.'

Sylvia was shaking now.

Donna was horrified. She'd somehow, without meaning to, without quite knowing why, she'd made her mum cry! For all the wrong reasons! Like there were right ones... You're not supposed to make your mum cry...

'I'm not gonna die, Mum! No policeman's gonna ring the doorbell and say I'm dead.'

'Why not?' Sylvia was almost screaming now, not in an angry way, but tears were rolling down her cheeks – no, they were actually throwing themselves down her face, like wet lemmings. 'Why not? It's what happened when your dad died!'

The sudden silence was gut-wrenchingly terrible.

Then Donna was across the room, hugging her sobbing mother, holding her, squeezing her, mumbling apologies and soothing words, telling her that it was all right, that she was there.

But one thought ran through her mind. Tomorrow, she'd be gone again. With the Doctor. Because that's what she wanted.

But did she have the right to? Had she really earned the right to go off again if this was what her mum thought?

All those times she and Sylvia had fought, argued, yelled. As a teenager (and frankly, most of her spoilt twenties), Donna had just put it down to 'that's my mum'. But Donna wasn't that person now, and she could see that her widowed mum, one year on, needed her daughter more than ever before.

And Donna was crying too now.

Crying for her mum's pain, her dad's loss, remembering that knock on the door. The policeman standing there.

'He was supposed to die here, in my arms, with his family,' Sylvia was saying. 'Not in a bloody filling station. Alone.'

At which point, with timing for which both the words 'impeccable' and 'inconvenient' were invented, the doorbell rang.

Wordlessly, Wilf went to answer it, and Donna heard him say 'Ah, not a good time.' Donna knew, without hearing the response, exactly who was on the doorstep.

And so did Sylvia.

She looked with red, teary eyes at her daughter.

And, for the first time that Donna could remember, Sylvia Noble stroked Donna's face, a soft caress of pure maternal love. 'I'll put the kettle on.' Then she called, 'Come in, Doctor.'

A moment later, the Doctor's face popped round the sitting room door, brainy specs in place, hair madder than normal.

'Hullo,' he said to all of them. 'Do you know the Carnes family by any chance? I think they've got aliens in the family.'

The tourist trade in Moscatelli was mainly based around olive groves, orangeries, a nice vineyard and the annual motorcycle race that started thirteen miles away in Florence and ended up the other side of the mountains in this small but oft-visited little town.

The people who lived in Moscatelli were mostly Italians who had been there for thirty or so generations. Everyone knew everyone and it was friendly, welcoming and cheerful.

It was also, in the middle of May, the recipient of stunningly good weather, and Jayne Greene thought it brought out the best in the locals. Not least of which was that Tonio was spending most of the day during the dig wearing nothing but a pair of tight denim cut-offs that left very little to the imagination (and Jayne could imagine quite a lot). The Professor had employed Tonio and his family to help them set up the dig a week or so back. Jayne and her two fellow students, Sean and Ben, had agreed to accompany the Professor there for the summer because it would give them really good marks in the end-of-course assessments, it'd be an adventure to travel to a nice part of Italy and it was a great way to get a tan.

'Got it!' Sean yelled excitedly.

'How much?' asked Ben, sifting soil a couple of feet away from where the laptop was set up by the food tent.

'Seventy-eight euro.'

'Sixty-something quid. Not bad.' Ben nodded. 'Well done.'

'I bloody love eBay,' Sean smiled at Jayne. 'Yaay me!'

'Was it the Egyptian pot?'

Sean looked at her and shook his head, slowly.

'Not the Iron Age spade?'

More head shaking.

Jayne dropped her own tools and wandered over to the laptop and looked at what Sean had just committed sixty pounds to.

'That?'

'That.'

'It's a toy.'

'Course it's a toy,' Ben yelled as Tonio poured some more earth into his sieve. 'What else does Sean ever buy off eBay?'

Jayne couldn't understand it. 'You mean, you spent all that money, and seven days' frustrated watching the auction, for a mass-produced toy?'

'Action figure,' Sean corrected her. 'Limited edition. Only five hundred produced, and that was eight years ago. It's a variant paint job, y'see, she's wearing her red Dark Period costume instead of the traditional green one.'

Jayne just looked at Sean. 'You are an adult. You are a grown man getting excited about a plastic toy. A figure for kids. A…'

'Don't say "dolly",' Ben muttered to himself.

'… a dolly?'

Sean slammed the laptop shut. 'My money, my choice. You get excited about Roman pins and earthenware.'

'So do you!'

'Yeah, cos that's a job. That's what I do here and at uni. But in my spare time, I have other hobbies. I have…'

'Don't say "a life",' Ben muttered to himself again.

'… a life,' Sean finished. 'You should try getting one before you criticise everyone else.'

Jayne stared at Sean, then across at Ben, who made sure he caught no one's eye and started to run his finger pointlessly through the dirt, in an effort to pretend he had something to distract him.

The tension was broken by little Professor Rossi, stumbling back around the tents after a trip to the town for some milk and teabags.

'Now, now, I could hear you up on the main road. What's going on?'

'Nothing,' Sean grunted. 'Sorry Prof.'

Rossi shook his head, scratching the scar that created a small slash across his cheek. At uni, everyone joked it was a duelling scar he'd got fighting for a woman he loved, but one day someone discovered the truth – that ten years earlier he'd been cut in the car accident that had killed his wife. Everyone lost interest in imagining romantic things about the scar after that.

'What am I going to do with you three? I bring you out here from university for the mid-term break, to visit the family home, and to give you all the chance to improve your frankly dodgy archaeology marks. And all you do is play with the broadband, flirt with poor Tonio there and embarrass him, or drink too much orange wine. You are here to work, you know. Being sociable is a pleasant side effect but not essential. What is essential, however, is teamwork. Sean and Jayne, I don't care if you can't get on, but you will work together. Jayne and Ben, I don't care if you want to fight over Tonio's attention, you will work together. Sean and Ben I don't care if you can drink one another under the table at night, provided you turn up fresh and able the next day. Is all that understood? I am not your parents but I am the man who will mark your end-of-term papers, and you would do well to remember that keeping me sweet is a positive move.' Rossi put some cartons of milk on the table next to the laptop. 'So, whose turn is it to make tea?'

Sean volunteered as Rossi scooped up the laptop. 'Hopefully the Bursar has forwarded some more funds to us so we can try and trace those tunnels through the hills across to the lake.'

'How far do your family go back here, Professor?' Jayne asked.

Rossi shrugged. 'I'm in the process of finding that out at the library. Certainly my paternal great-grandparents were the ones who moved to Ipswich, but I suspect their roots are here right back to the fifteenth century.'

Ben headed over with his sieve. 'So we are looking for more than fifteenth-century Italian pots and pans then? I said so! Come on, Professor, what's the big secret?'

'Ah,' Rossi grinned. 'Well, you see, somewhere in this area an entire Dukedom vanished. A whole town with a castle and everything was based around here, or in the hills or somewhere in the vicinity of that lake beyond the orange groves. I'm trying to find its borders.'

'How do we know?' Sean asked as the kettle boiled.

'It's in the records in the library,' Tonio said in good but heavily accented English.

Jayne and Ben stared at Tonio in mute shock – and slight horror.

He grinned. 'Oh right, you both thought I didn't understand English,' he laughed, a deep bellowing laugh.

So did Professor Rossi. 'Now that,' he said, 'is funny. Did neither of you realise?'

Dumbly, they both shook their heads as Sean busied himself with the tea, determined not to catch their eyes.

'But that means…' Jayne started.

'Everything we've said…' added Ben.

'About you…' Jayne again.

'You… you heard… Oh God… kill me now…' Ben put his sieve down and sat hard on the ground.

Tonio tousled Ben's dark hair and winked at him, before throwing a look to Jayne. 'Sorry, you lose.'

'Course I do,' Jayne said. 'When does life ever go Jayne Greene's way?'

The laptop bleeped and, leaving the students to sort out the tea and Tonio's confession, Professor Rossi accessed his emails in response. Nothing from the Bursar, but there was one message:

From: Madam Delphi
To: *Rossi@Tarminsteruni.ac.uk*
Subject: SAN MARTINO

Professor Rossi

My congratulations, you have rediscovered your heritage, and you are indeed in San Martino, just as you hoped. Click on this <u>link</u> to be taken to my site for more information about this delightful Italianate kingdom and its secrets.

The Professor was about to call the students over, but thought it would be better to check that this wasn't a hoax. (Although how did anyone know they were searching for San Martino? He hadn't even told the students the name of the kingdom). So he clicked the hotlink.

Instead of a new webpage, the screen was instantly filled with a pulsating ball of bright white light, highlighted with lilac edges and spirals.

Instinctively he let his hand reach forward to touch the screen… to go into the screen, to go through the screen… as if his right hand was being consumed by the transfixing ball of energy.

Then he withdrew his hand, and looked at it.

Crackling around the fingertips were the vestiges of purple pulses of energy, like tiny flickers of raw electrical power. He turned his hand over, studying the little pulses until they seemed to vanish for good, absorbed into his skin. He rubbed his fingers together, and then looked back at the screen. It just displayed Sean's eBay victory again.

The Professor stood up and turned to face his students and held his arms out, hands flat. 'We've done it,' he breathed.

Instantly distracted from their own petty concerns, the four young people walked over, Jayne and Sean taking an offered hand each, excitedly returning the gesture, if unsure what they were celebrating.

After a second, they wordlessly released the Professor's hands, and Rossi then grabbed Ben and Tonio's hands. And they in turn took Sean and Jayne's, the five now forming a circle.

In unison, they all raised their linked hands into the air, purple electricity building and crackling around them.

The others followed the direction of his gaze as the Professor looked up into the sky.

'Welcome back,' he said quietly.

Dinner was subdued in the Noble household.

Sylvia silently put food on plates. Donna silently passed the plates from the work surface to the dining table. Wilf silently poured water into tumblers – three matching ones from a petrol station, and a larger one with Donald Duck on it. The Doctor had that.

The Doctor sat there, uncomfortable with domesticity at the best of times, utterly ill at ease right now.

'Dubai?' Sylvia said, suddenly sitting up.

The Doctor shot a look at Donna – what was he supposed to say?

'With the horses,' Wilf helpfully prodded.

'Horses?' The Doctor was like a rabbit caught in headlights. 'Horses. Yes, marvellous things.'

'The Sheikh of Dubai put us up for a couple of weeks,' Donna interjected. '*Didn't* he?'

Sylvia started eating. Something cheese-y and macaroni-y the Doctor had guessed, but he wasn't quite sure. Something that looked like this had once tried to bite off his toes on the coast of Kal-Durunt in the Keripedes Cluster.

He gently eased his fork into it.

'I'm sorry it's not as posh as what you get in Dubai, with horses and sheikhs,' Sylvia said. 'But I had no notice from either of you that you were coming.'

'Oh, well, we couldn't have Donna missing today,' the Doctor said brightly. Too brightly. Wrong occasion for Tigger-Doctor, better to be Eeyore-Doctor tonight.

'I thought the Emirates were run by emirs, not sheikhs,' Sylvia said, pouring herself more water. 'But what do I know? I just sit here every day, waiting for people to turn up out of the blue, expecting to be fed.'

The Doctor just threw a look at Donna that he thought said 'help' but Donna clearly took to mean 'no, it's OK, ignore me, oh and right now would be the time to pick a really good fight with your mum'.

So Donna did.

'What is your problem, Mum? Most people would kill to have family around them.'

Wilf tried to intervene, but Donna was going off on one now.

'I mean, Mooky goes away for two weeks, her parents throw a bloody party to celebrate her return. And all she's done is go shopping in Glasgow. I get to see the gala- well, to see the world, things I never thought I'd get the chance to do, and all I get is moans.'

Sylvia didn't look up from her food. 'Yeah, but they probably knew where Mooky was. All I know is when your granddad there bothers to say he had a postcard. And I'm never allowed to read them, oh no.'

Donna was going to chastise Wilf for that when she remembered that said postcards were usually sent from another star system entirely.

'OK, Mum, I'll start sending you postcards too. Promise.'

'Oh it's not just that,' Sylvia said. 'It's the whole life I have. Your dad's gone, you've gone, and I'm stuck here as nursemaid for your granddad's bit on the side.'

Donna opened her mouth to speak, then shut it again. Then, as that comment sank in, her mouth opened again, but still no sound came out.

'Bit on the side?' the Doctor asked Wilf.

Wilf glowered at Sylvia. 'She's a friend,' he said. 'I'm not gonna marry her.'

'I should hope not,' Sylvia said. 'Mum would turn in her grave.'

'Ahhh, so that's what it's all about,' Wilf sighed. 'You think Eileen wouldn't approve. You think somehow me seeing a poor, sick old lady would make Eileen sad. Well, you're wrong. She was your mother, but she was my wife. I knew her better than that.'

The Doctor remembered why he didn't 'do' families.

'Lovely macaroni cheese, Mrs Noble,' he said, stuffing his mouth. 'Mmmmm…'

'It's mushroom raclette,' she snapped.

'Not macaroni?'

'Mushroom.'

'It's… great… very cheesy. And…'

'So, who is this lady, Gramps?' Donna asked.

Wilf smiled. 'She's a lady astronomer I know, from Greenwich. Helps out at the observatory there, has done for years. But about three years ago she was… well, she fell ill and had to stop working. We chatted on the phone a couple of times, met up, had dinner. You'd think I'd started dating a teenage married pregnant cousin the way Sylvia goes on about her.'

The Doctor was looking at Sylvia Noble, however. Spotting what made her flush angrily when Wilf spoke. It had been the word 'ill'.

He looked back at the old paratrooper. 'Why'd she give up at the Observatory then?'

'Ask her yourself,' Sylvia said. 'She'll be here any minute. Even on Geoff's day, my daughter brings *you* round, and he brings *her* round.'

And Sylvia was up and out of the kitchen.

Donna sighed and went after her mum. Wilf made to follow, but the Doctor caught his arm.

'I'm no expert, Wilfred, but I reckon best leave the ladies to it.'

Wilf nodded.

'And your friend?'

'Netty. Henrietta Goodhart.'

He smiled. 'Most appropriate name I think she could have. But she was diagnosed with... She has Alzheimer's, Doctor. And it's not getting any better.'

'It wouldn't,' the Doctor said quietly, just as the doorbell rang. 'That her?'

Wilf nodded and went to let her in.

A moment later and the Doctor was grinning at a vision of eccentricity, charm and humour that only certain English women of a particular age and bearing could carry off.

She was dressed from head to foot in brown – knee-length corduroy skirt, tan blouse, chocolate-coloured jacket – and carried a tan handbag. On her head was an amazing hat with at least half a dozen brown feathers of different shapes and sizes. Wilf was removing her long dark overcoat, and Netty offered her hand to the Doctor before Wilf had got the coat off her, meaning one sleeve, the hand-shaking sleeve, was still on.

'Doctor, how marvellous to meet you. Hooray and huzzah, it's a real pleasure.'

'Mrs Goodhart.'

'Miss, please. Better still, just Netty. Never been married and, despite what Wilfred's daughter believes, have no intention to ever be married.'

Wilf finally got the coat off her, and Netty slid neatly into a chair, grabbing a glass of water in an obviously well-rehearsed manoeuvre.

'I never married,' she went on. 'Seemed such an alarming waste of time. I live in Greenwich you know, bit of a trek out here, but my local cab firm, they know me and my little ways, so it's never a problem if I forget to have money. Or where I'm going.'

The Doctor had taken to this gregarious lady instantly. 'You can't beat a reliable taxi firm, Netty,' he said, managing to get a sentence in before she blithely carried on.

'Are they rowing yet? It's all they ever do. And it's about me. I was so ashamed to start with, now I just treat it as a ritual, and in ten minutes Sylvia's back to her normal charming self, full of tea and crackers.'

The Doctor smiled. 'Sylvia Noble? Charming? Words not often in the same sentence.'

The look he got from Netty showed him how he'd misjudged the situation between the two women.

'Oh, don't disappoint me, Doctor. Not after all I've been told about you. That woman out there is a saint. She's just lost her husband, she's got a daughter you drag halfway to God knows where on a whim, and has to tolerate that marvellous Wilfred, who can be just as stubborn and cantankerous as her. More so in fact. I like her a lot. Besides which, and I know she complains, but that's just her way of letting off steam, she's bloody terrific with my... you know...' Netty tapped the side of her head. 'My condition. Bless her, last weekend she drove Wilf all the way to Charlton. Apparently I was found in someone's back garden, trying to convince them I used to live there when I was six!'

'And did you?'

'Good gracious, no. I was brought up in Hampshire.' She dived into her handbag and brought out an A5-sized red notebook and showed it to him. 'My life,' she said simply. 'So I can remember things.'

The Doctor looked her straight in the eye and saw, briefly, a very scared but very proud old lady. And he liked her even more than before.

'Without that book, without the likes of Sylvia Noble, I'm nothing. I'd left my bag in a shop on Greenwich High Street, so I'm in this garden, unable to know who I am, where I'm from. Sylvia found a receipt in my pocket, found the shop, got my bag back from where I'd left it, sorted it all out with the police. She wants to put me in a home, you know. The brochures are in that drawer next to the cooker.'

'Really?'

'Yes. Wilf won't hear of it. Says he'll have me move in here first. Daft old fool, as if I'm going to go from one house I can barely cope with to another. But a lovely nursing home, where I'll be looked after? How marvellous is that?'

The kitchen door opened. Donna and Sylvia trooped in, and Donna immediately introduced herself.

As Sylvia put the kettle on, the Doctor crossed and stood behind her. 'Does Wilf know all you do for his friend?'

'Does Donna know you're poking your nose into her family's business?' Sylvia responded.

'I'm not your enemy, Mrs Noble,' the Doctor said.

Sylvia turned and smiled at him. The most insincere

smile possible. 'For my daughter's sake, Doctor, I tolerate you in this house. But that's all. For my dad's sake, I'll do the best I can for Netty Goodhart. I don't think I'm a selfish woman, Doctor. I've worked hard, I built a life, I never had much money, and I tried to give Donna a decent life. But then one day, I lost my husband. My rock. And since then I've tried to do what both of us did, but with a daughter who one minute won't get a job, the next can afford to be in a different hemisphere, but can't afford a stamp, and an old dad who seems to have decided it's time to replace my mum once and for all.'

'Are you sure you're not worried he's replacing you? I imagine he let your mum go a long time ago.'

The silence that followed the slap around the face he received seemed to go on for a few hours, but was probably only a few seconds.

'I didn't mean it like that…' the Doctor started. 'I genuinely wondered—'

Sylvia ignored him. 'Dad,' she said. 'Why don't you take the Doctor up to the allotment, eh? Donna and I can catch up with Netty while you two have an hour or… a few hours up there, yes?'

Wilf took the hint and was all but dragging the Doctor out of the kitchen as the women watched.

The last thing the Doctor heard was 'Tea, everyone' from Sylvia, before Wilf had thrust them both out into the night air.

'Allotment. This way,' the old man said.

Babis Takis hoiked the largest bale of hay onto the back of the station wagon and stopped to rest. He wasn't getting any younger, and this was really Nikos's job.

But Nikos wasn't here, he was probably around the back of the farm, messing with that Spiros girl. Typical. There was work to be done – they had to get this consignment over to Faliraki, where so much building work was still going on. Hotels, apartments, shopping malls, everything the whole Dodecanese would benefit from because of the continued tourism it would bring.

Babis yelled out Nikos's name a couple of times as he hauled up more bales of hay. He glanced at his watch. It would take an hour or so to drive across the island to the Petaloudes, where they would collect Kris, before going on to Lindos and along the coast to Faliraki. They'd drop off the hay at the depot, then it was off to Erik's Taverna for the night.

Still no sign of Nikos.

With a sigh, Babis walked away from the station wagon. 'I am an old man, Nikos,' he called out. 'I fought in the war, you know, so people like you could be independent and have your luxuries. Just once, it'd be nice if you could pull your weight.'

He had reached the rear of the farm, when he heard a noise from inside one of the stables – a short female gasp of surprise, almost fear. Certainly alarm.

Babis was inside the stable in a second.

Nikos was on the ground, holding his head in his hands, silent but clearly dazed.

Standing over him, a shovel in her hands was a pretty young girl, who Babis recognised as Katarina Spiros.

'You all right, girl?' Babis asked, reaching for the shovel.

Katarina swung around to face Nikos's grandfather, and he realised how scared she looked. 'What happened?' Babis asked.

He was surprised when Katarina explained. 'He took a call…'

She was pointing at Nikos Takis, who was now beginning to stand up, abandoning the cell phone on the ground by his foot. He looked at his grandfather, causing Babis to take an involuntary step back.

Babis Takis had fought in the latter days of the war as a youth, kicking the Nazis out of Crete and keeping Greece for the Greeks. He had faced the wrath and pain of his parents, who had so hated and eventually rejected him for falling in love, marrying and having children with one of the hated Italians who had occupied the Greek Islands for seven hundred years before being sent packing after the war. He had done some time in prison for a bar-room brawl in Diagoras, and he had once had to face the embittered son of a German he'd tied a live grenade to back in 1944.

But nothing had ever scared him as much as the look his grandson gave him right now.

Nikos wasn't there any more. That carefree, funny, clever grandson he had nurtured after his father's death was just not there.

Babis didn't know how he knew that. He didn't know how it had happened. But he'd never been so sure of anything in his life.

He was still sure of this when a flash of purple fire, hotter than the heart of a sun, extinguished his existence in less time than it took Katarina Spiros to draw breath to scream.

A second later, a handful of ashes dropped to the ground where the young girl had stood.

And Nikos Takis threw his arms towards the sky, purple electricity buzzing around his fingertips, as he threw back his head.

'Welcome back,' he yelled triumphantly.

Donnie and Portia were on their honeymoon. It was Donnie's first, Portia's second, but both were enjoying themselves enormously.

Donnie's son had been his best man. His grandson had been pageboy. Portia's granddaughter had been the flower-girl. They'd had two ceremonies, a full-on Jewish one and a simpler Christian one to reflect both their chosen faiths. Portia had always stayed in the Jewish faith, whereas Donnie's family had pretty much abandoned it within weeks of arriving at Ellis Island a century and a bit earlier.

They had overcome the odds – a cancer scare for Donnie, some severe frowning by Portia's more traditional relatives and the death of their 8-year-old cat, Mr Smokey, a week before the ceremonies. After knowing each other for fifteen years, courting for the last six, they were finally together for ever.

And here they were, in Donnie's jeep, having bombed along the 8, passing through Danbury, before turning off the freeway and into the Connecticut countryside for their honeymoon.

They had taken a nice colonial house outside Olivertown, thirteen miles from Danbury. The house belonged to one of Portia's clients (she was a dog-walker, traipsing three times a day around Central Park with a variety of canines). The Carpenters were on FM radio, telling the world how they'd like to teach the world to sing, and the happy couple were singing along.

They'd got through Abba, Dr Hook and the Medicine Show, Jo Stafford, and were nodding their heads gently along to Helen Reddy singing about how good it was to be insane: 'No one asks you to explain' they sang in unison as they pulled up outside the house they'd rented.

Portia looked at her new husband. 'Well, Mr DiCotta, we're here.'

'We sure are, Mrs DiCotta.' Donnie winked at her. 'Gotten used to that yet?'

'Never will, I reckon,' she laughed. 'But I like it just the same.' She leaned across the car and kissed Donnie as he switched the ignition off.

And the radio kept playing.

As they separated, they both looked at the fascia of the stereo.

'That's not good, Donnie,' Portia DiCotta said. 'Must be a short somewhere.'

He nodded. 'Darn it, I'd better get it fixed up now, hon. Otherwise we'll have a flat battery tomorrow which would not be good as I want to take you up to that restaurant in New Preston. The food's gorgeous, the hospitality's first class and the view is to die for. You can look right down over Lake Waramaug and it's real romantic.'

Portia nodded. 'You sort the car, I'll put some coffee on.'

Donnie reached out to feel under the dash for a loose wire. There was a tiny spark of electricity and the radio fell silent.

'Well done you.' Portia smiled. 'Now you can help me get the cases out the back.'

Donnie DiCotta said nothing. He just kept his hand under the dashboard of the jeep, staring ahead.

'Donnie?'

Nothing.

Portia reached out to touch his shoulder, and he swung his head round to face her. Portia saw his eyes – not the beautiful blue eyes that she'd fallen in love with. These had been replaced by two solid orbs of burning purple light, minuscule tongues of electricity sparking from his tear ducts.

She couldn't say a word because he grabbed her head and kissed her on the mouth. Full. Hard. But not at all passionate.

After a second or two, they broke apart.

And now Portia DiCotta's eyes were blazing with the same eerie purple energy.

Wordlessly, they got out of the jeep and walked to the porch, studying the night sky above them, until Donnie pointed up to the right, to a blazing star that, had he been an expert in such things, he'd have known hadn't been seen by human eyes for many centuries.

He and his new wife held hands and stared at the star.

'Welcome back,' they breathed together.

*

The Doctor was looking down on London.

'I can see why you like it up here, Wilf,' he said to the old man fussing beside him, sorting out a second little canvas seat for him to sit on. 'It's terribly... peaceful.'

Wilf Mott nodded. 'Been coming here for years. Used to stare at the sky at night when I was in the forces. Used to navigate by the stars as well as the charts and stuff. The other lads thought I was mad, but you know what, Doctor, we never got lost. Not once.'

The Doctor smiled at the older man and sat on the proffered seat. 'Thank you.'

Wilf sat beside him and poured him a mug of tea from the thermos. The Doctor sipped it gratefully. 'Used to slip a bit of Mr Daniels' finest in there,' Wilf said. 'But her ladyship cottoned on and that was the end of that. Bleedin' doctors told her I had to keep off it.'

'Terrible bunch, doctors,' the Doctor laughed. 'But they often know what's best, however unpopular that makes them.'

'Subtle,' nodded Wilf. 'Sylv'll come round. Probably.'

'Really?'

'Nah,' and Wilf roared. 'Not a chance, mate.'

The Doctor smiled again. 'You don't have a problem with me, then?'

'Oh, you make my Donna happy. Keep that up and you're fine with me. Do anything that upsets her, though, and you'll hear from me, even on Mars.'

The Doctor looked surprised at this. 'How much has she told you?'

'Everything. Right from the off.' Wilf pointed at his

telescope. 'I was up here, looking up into the sky when she told me about you. I didn't believe her at first.'

'Well, no one could blame you for that.'

'Truth is, I don't think I understood what she was actually telling me. Then I saw you after that fat business, flying through the sky, Donna waving down at me, and I realised it was all true. She keeps me up to date when she can. Postcards, emails. The odd gift. Still don't know what to do with the Verron medal. Or what exactly a Verron medal is!'

The Doctor grinned. 'Marvellous race, Verrons. They have a brilliant air corps. Utterly useless, they haven't fought a war in a few millennia, but their air corps is their proudest achievement. It's a bit like you sending someone a three-bar DSO.' The Doctor shrugged. 'Hang on, when did she send you that, where did she get it from, and how on earth did she get it to you?'

Wilf almost recoiled from the Doctor's stream-of-conscious barrage of questions.

'Not a clue. 'Ere, you don't need it back, do you? I mean, it wasn't stolen? Donna hasn't nicked anything since those sweets from Woolies when she was eight. We made her take 'em back and apologise and everything.'

'No, no, I doubt she nicked it. Verrons are very generous. I just want to know when she met a Verron.'

'I'd hate to think my little girl was not being properly looked after, Doctor,' Wilf said, raising an eyebrow.

'Helios 5,' the Doctor said. 'Had to be there. Or Ylum. I like Ylum, so did Donna – very cosmopolitan. Or perhaps from the *Moulin Très Rouge*. There was a street market there. Or I suppose there was that day on—'

'Anyway,' Wilf cut across him, 'we came here for a reason.'

'A reason other than you wanting to check what my intentions were towards your granddaughter? And to give my left cheek a chance to cool down.'

Wilf laughed. 'Oh, that's Sylvia's way, not mine. I know you're honourable. I also know Donna can take care of herself in that regard. Any dishonourability from you, you'd never hear the end of it. Literally.'

The Doctor thought about 'oi' and decided yes, Wilf knew his granddaughter very well indeed.

Wilf adjusted his telescope. 'Look though here.'

The Doctor did, and saw a star. A tiny little pinprick of light, flickering enough that every so often it seemed to vanish.

'Like it? 7432MOTT,' Wilf said proudly.

'I'm sorry,' the Doctor said, staring back at him again. 'They named it after you?'

'I discovered it. I joined a node. Not long after, I discovered that star. The RPS are doing me a dinner tomorrow night.'

'I node nudding anout nodes,' the Doctor said.

'Ah, well a node is—' Wilf started, but the Doctor waved it aside.

'I'm joking. I know what a node is. And I'm dead impressed, Wilf, that you have a star named in your honour and I'm even more overjoyed the Royal Planetary Society are throwing you a knees-up. And I bet you bought a new tie and everything. And I am so sorry to have to rain on your parade, but can I just point out that there's *another* new star, just down there. It's incredibly bright, just to the left of the sword of Orion.'

Wilf leaned down and eased the Doctor aside. 'There?'

'No, *there*.'

'Oh, there. Yeah, we all like that one, too. It's very pretty.'

'Yeah, very pretty. A very pretty new star shining brightly in a constellation that it shouldn't be anywhere near. Thing is, stars of that magnitude and shininess don't just show up for no good reason.'

'Shininess? Is that a technical term?'

The Doctor threw Wilf a look. 'It's good enough for me.'

'Only I know that everyone who's been talking about it calls stars like that Chaos Bodies, apparently.'

The Doctor thought for a second or two, then shrugged. 'Do they? That's a new one on me.'

'It's what they called it in the papers.'

The Doctor nodded. 'Ah, well, if the newspapers said it, it must be true, because who on earth would argue with the tabloids.' He looked up at the thing in the sky. 'Chaos Bodies. Good descriptive name though, they got that right.' The Doctor threw an arm around Wilf's shoulder. 'But you know what, who cares? You got a star, a much less worrying star, named after you and I'm very proud.'

'Thank you. I'm glad you said that cos you have just solved my problem for me.'

'What problem is that?'

'I need someone to take me to Vauxhall.'

'Why?'

'The dinner.'

'Who with?'

'The Society.'

'When?'

'Tomorrow night.'

'How?'

'By TARDIS?'

'Yeah, cos *that's* gonna happen.'

'Well all right, on the tube, then. Sylvia thinks I'm not capable of going by myself. I mean, I'm fine sitting in a cold, damp allotment every night, which plays havoc with my—'

'So Sylvia doesn't want you going out late at night, right?'

'I mean, I'm not gonna get lost, Doctor, but she's getting all protective and daft these days. Since she lost Geoff. And with Donna away so much. And now Netty…'

'You know what, Wilfred Mott, I should be delighted to accompany you to dinner in Vauxhall. By taxi – how posh is that? I haven't had a meal at the RPS since Bernard and Paula took me there in 1969 to watch the moon landings. Do they still do that chocolate syrup pudding?'

'I don't know. I haven't been before.'

'Then tomorrow night, Wilfred Mott of Chiswick, assuming the menu hasn't changed in forty years, and being the Royal Planetary Society I think I'm on safe ground there, you are in for a culinary treat.'

The Doctor looked at the worryingly bright new star that wasn't 7432MOTT one last time through the telescope. 'Chaos Body indeed.'

'It is beautiful, though,' Wilf murmured.

And both men suddenly shivered. Like someone was walking over their graves.

Or the grave of the entire planet.

'Beautiful Chaos,' the Doctor said quietly.

SATURDAY

Caitlin stood waiting at Heathrow Airport, Terminal 5, waiting for flights that would once have gone into Terminal 2. That was currently being demolished, ready for the East Terminal that would replace the one European flights used to come into. She was meeting various inbound flights, including one due in from JFK at midday, which would arrive before the European ones. She watched the huge 787-9 jet come in to land, sunlight gleaming off its new fuselage as it slowly crawled to a halt, before taxiing across to the arrival gate and being drawn into position by the small pilot truck.

Caitlin was dressed in a smart Terminal Staff uniform, her access-all-areas pass, with the highest security clearing Madam Delphi could get, dangling from the strap around her neck. She smiled sweetly at a couple of other staff, neither of whom challenged her even though they couldn't possibly have ever seen her before. It was the pass that did that, although Caitlin's long dark hair and blue eyes would have been enough to distract anyone who wanted a closer look. A quick smile was usually all it took Caitlin to get exactly what she wanted.

It was actually a keen security guard who spotted her

as she walked through Restricted Access doors towards the arrivals lounge, heading to exactly where she really had no right to be.

'Excuse me?' he called out.

'Is there a problem…' Caitlin screwed up her eyes to read his name tag. 'Is there a problem, Keith?'

Keith Brownlow stared at her, his head slightly to one side as if sizing her up. 'Not seen you before,' he said quietly.

'Not been here long,' she answered quickly.

'Funny,' he replied. 'I know everyone in this Terminal. And those I don't know, don't get in here. I need you to leave, I'm afraid, until I can verify you are who you say you are.'

Caitlin paused for a moment, trying to remember a name. 'I'm sure if you check with Mr Golding he'll vouch for me. I joined his staff on Thursday.'

Keith shrugged. 'And I'll do that, but only once you go back the way you came and wait in the Yellow Zone.'

'You're very good at this, Keith, aren't you?'

'We take security very seriously,' he said.

'Of course you do,' purred Caitlin. 'Quite right too. But look, there's only you and me here, you've seen my pass, you can see I have clearance. I'm sure it's just administration that have failed to inform you I'm here. I really need to be the other side of that door to greet some VIPs.'

Keith ignored her, his right hand resting on the holstered revolver at his hip, his left hand raising his walkie-talkie.

'Oh dear, and I thought we might become friends,'

Caitlin said, raising her right arm and sending a bolt of purple energy into Keith's chest, reducing him to ashes before he could even register the movement.

She walked forward, her high heels squashing the few ashes that remained into the carpet. With a quick, deep breath, she pushed open the VIP area doors and marched out to greet her guests.

They were standing, waiting for her, neither of them really seeming to register where they were or what they were doing. Two old Americans, in from New York.

'Mr and Mrs DiCotta? Congratulations on your wedding and welcome to your honeymoon.'

Donnie and Portia DiCotta said nothing, just nodded as Caitlin led them to one of the service buggies that elderly and disabled passengers were moved around the airport terminals in.

A confused handler looked at her pass as she flashed it at him, but then moved on, allowing her to take the buggy. The DiCottas climbed on board as the handler turned back.

'Do they have luggage?' he called out.

Caitlin smiled her sweetest smile, which she hoped didn't suggest what she thought ('Oh, do go away, you pointless oaf'), then said aloud, 'It's been delayed at JFK so we'll come back for it in the morning.'

She started the buggy up and drove forward. 'You're the first,' she said quietly, no longer all sweetness and smiles.

'Where are the others?'

'The Greek is in shortly, the Italian group, not for another hour or so. We'll wait, collect them and then go to Madam Delphi together. She has a mission for you tonight.' Caitlin gave a little laugh. 'I would ask about jetlag, but I imagine Madam Delphi has ensured you feel none of that.'

'We feel fine,' said Portia DiCotta.

'Good,' Caitlin said. 'Perfect.'

The buggy carried on, away from the main routes and across to another Gate where the flight from Athens International would arrive. 'And then we're off to meet the funky 787-3 from Aeroporto Leonardo da Vinci di Fiumicino,' she said. 'I do hope you enjoy your stay. It'll be brief but very dramatic.'

The little buggy trundled on down the long corridors ready to collect more of the army that Madam Delphi would eventually use to bring the human race to utter destruction.

Donna was adjusting the Doctor's tie. She'd done this a hundred times for her dad, especially towards the end, which had given him an excuse to be grouchy and feel useless. The Doctor had no such excuse, but it hadn't stopped him moaning about it.

'Donna, I can tie a tie, you know.'

'Really? Cos I've seen no evidence of that,' was her response, followed by an overenthusiastic shove of the knot a bit too close to the Doctor's Adam's apple. 'Whoops,' she smiled at him. 'So sorry.'

He slid a finger down his shirt collar and somehow that single gesture seemed not only to loosen the knot, but also to undo his top button and then put creases into the shirt as well.

It was an art, he said. Geek chic, he said. Scruffy Arthur, she called it, giving up on a lost cause.

'How's Netty getting on?' he asked.

'She's OK today,' Donna said. 'Granddad's fussing round her. Mum's speaking through gritted teeth because of it, so Netty's hopped off early and said she'll meet us there. I reckon she's gone to buy another daft hat!'

'Your mum's worried about Wilf, that's all. Netty's great fun but a big responsibility,' the Doctor said.

'I know, but Mum doesn't have to be so negative about it, does she?'

The Doctor shrugged. 'She's a mum, Donna. It's their job to find fault with everyone in their family. It's in the handbook.'

'Did your mum criticise everything you do? The way you brushed your hair, the clothes you wore, the friends you hung out with, the music—'

'Yeah, well, it was a bit different for me,' he said quietly.

Donna looked at him and smiled comfortingly. 'Of course it was. Sorry. Didn't think.'

'Oh, it's all right. I'm just saying, give your mum some credit. It's a lot to cope with – she's looked after your granddad alone for a long time. Now he has someone in his life, she's bound to be a bit put out.'

'Oh don't go all Spock on me.'

'Spock?'

'Yeah, child psychologist blokey, or whatever he was. All about relations between parents and kids.'

'Ah. Dr Spock. Right.'

'Why, is there another Spock that you know?' laughed Donna as she headed out of the spare room. Although she suspected the Doctor hadn't slept a wink in there – he never seemed to need sleep like a normal person.

The Doctor glanced at himself in the mirror. He always thought he looked quite good in a dinner jacket and black tie – he hated bow ties, they made him look like a waiter, going by what had happened at other parties, so tonight it was a black tie proper. Course, it meant he now looked like he was going to a funeral, but hey-ho. And what was it with jackets, no matter how he buttoned them up, they always looked like they were too small or too tight, and the trousers never quite reached down to his ankles.

Ah well, it was Wilf's night, not his.

There was a knock on the door. 'Yeah, I'm coming, Donna, give us a minute.'

The door opened. It was Donna's mum.

'Ah. Hullo,' he said. She was an intimidating woman and, like most mothers, she clearly didn't like him much. Was he imagining it or was his cheek starting to ache again?

Some mothers he could win over by sheer charm (ah, Jackie Tyler, what are you doing these days?), or by proving that their daughter's faith in him was justified (still got a good right hook, Francine Jones, bless you).

Now there was Sylvia Noble. Full of so much pride, tempered with so much rage, so much frustration. It was as if she never felt quite so in control of her life as she told herself she was, and that made her really angry.

Of course, it couldn't have been easy losing Geoff.

The Doctor had only met him once, at Donna's wedding, where he seemed to be the more… temperate of the Noble parents. Now poor Sylvia was trying her best to deal with a wayward daughter who was nowhere near as wayward as Sylvia imagined (she still had no idea where he really took Donna) and an elderly father, who was so determined not to be a burden on his daughter that he became a bigger one by default. Wilf Mott wanted to prove he was independent, strong and twenty years younger than he was, believing it would take pressure off Sylvia; he just didn't realise that Sylvia saw through this and was twice as worried as she would be if he just sat in an armchair all day watching *Countdown*.

How long was it since the Doctor had sat down and watched *Countdown*? He used to like *Countdown*.

'You'll take care of him.'

'You're not coming with us?'

Sylvia looked as if she was about to say something, but then she just shook her head slightly. 'Not my thing.'

'But it's your dad…'

'We had a… discussion about that.'

'Ah.' The Doctor could only begin to imagine how that went. 'Are you sure? Because I'm positive he, Donna and Netty would love you–'

He stopped. Sylvia was one step away from flinching at the mention of Henrietta Goodhart.

'Look after him, please, Doctor,' she said quietly. 'He's not getting any younger, despite what he thinks.'

The Doctor smiled disarmingly. 'Course I will.'

'There's no "course I will" about it with you, Doctor,

so don't give me any of your so-called charm and flannel. I wasn't asking a question, I was telling you.'

The Doctor tried not to smile – it was like being told off by a headmistress. Then the glint in Sylvia's eye reminded him this was not remotely funny.

'Promise,' he said, mentally adding, 'And I'll do three hundred lines: "I will not lose members of the Noble family in London".'

'They're all I have,' she said and walked out of the room.

The Doctor licked his forefinger and held it up.

Yup, the room's ambient temperature had indeed dropped several degrees.

Half an hour later, they had piled into a cab. Wilf and Donna sat on the seat, the Doctor on one of those fold-down spare seats. He wriggled uncomfortably on it for the whole journey.

Wilf was dressed up to the nines – silk tie, good shirt, slightly tight jacket that had probably been bought in the early seventies – but was let down by the pair of trainers on his feet.

As if sensing where the Doctor was looking, Wilf held up a tatty carrier bag. Inside it was a pair of black dress shoes. 'They don't half kill the circulation in my feet, so I wear 'em as little time as I can,' he explained.

The Doctor nodded. 'You look nice,' he said to Donna.

'Thanks. Had to borrow something off of Veena, who'd lent it to Mooky, so she had to bring it round this afternoon while you were out getting your suit and – what?'

The Doctor grinned. 'Your friends have amazing names.' He laughed gently. 'Mooky.'

Donna raised an eyebrow at this. 'You can talk. Mister Ood. Mister Matron Cofelia. Mister Ventraxian Gol-Zeeglar. Where d'you get off thinking my mates' names are funny-sounding, eh?'

'Fair point, although Ood isn't really a name, it's more a sort of species designation, and I… um…'

Donna was giving him one of her 'do I look like I care' looks, so he turned to Wilf instead.

'Excited?'

'Too right I am, Doctor. I get a star to myself. Named after me. How great is that?'

'It's more than great, Gramps,' Donna squeezed his hand. 'It's bloody marvellous. Spaceman over there, ask him if anyone's named a star after him.'

'Have they, Doctor?'

Whether they had or hadn't was neither here nor there right now. 'Absolutely not,' he told Wilf. 'And I'm very jealous.'

'Yeah,' Wilf leaned forward, so the driver wouldn't hear him. 'Yeah, but you? You get to visit 'em, don't you? You get to go up there.' He turned to Donna and nudged her playfully. 'You make the most of it, my girl.'

'Oh, I am, don't you worry,' she said.

The Doctor nodded. 'Oh, she is, don't you worry at all.'

'I mean, I've seen and done some things in my time, Doctor, but nothing can compare to what you're showing my little girl, eh?'

'Hey, I'm not just a passenger, you know,' Donna

smiled. 'I get to make a lot of the decisions about where we go, who we see, how quickly we have to leave again, cos he's gone and upset someone in charge. With an army. And a big axe. And twelve legs.'

'Ten legs,' the Doctor automatically corrected her.

'Oooh, all right then. Ten legs, and two arms that hung down to the ground. If you're being pedantic. Which you clearly are. Tonight.'

The Doctor grinned at them both. 'Maybe we should take you with us on a jaunt one day, Wilf.'

'No!'

Both Donna and Wilf had said that together, then looked at each other.

'It's dangerous, Granddad.'

'You go!'

'I'm... I can look after myself. If anything happened to you, what'd Mum do?'

'Kill you?'

'Well, she'd kill him,' Donna nodded at the Doctor. 'I'd get away with being skinned alive. Probably.'

'You said "no" too, Wilf,' the Doctor said.

Wilf looked up at the stars as they drove into South London, crossing Vauxhall Bridge. 'I like to look, Doctor. I like to look, and imagine and dream. But the reality? All them monsters and guns and stuff? Nah. I prefer my ideas.'

The Doctor nodded. 'Very wise. Mind you, you'd be a calming influence on her.'

'Oh I know. She does go on, doesn't she?'

'I am sitting here. Right here,' Donna said.

The Doctor was still talking to Wilf. 'And there's

obviously something in her childhood about centipedes, but she won't say what. Cos we went to this one place—'

'Oi!'

Wilf laughed. 'Oh, I gotta tell you about that. When she was about eight, her dad and I took her up Norfolk way. To the Broads? Anyway, she was paddling about when—'

'*OI!!*'

They both looked at Donna. She was pointing to herself. One finger on each hand. At her head.

'As I said. Sat here. Listening. *Not* liking.'

The two men grinned at each other.

'Later,' the Doctor said.

'Later,' Wilf confirmed.

Donna broke them up. 'We're here.'

The cab pulled up outside the Society, a huge red-brick building built in early Victorian times, just off the main circus by Vauxhall station.

Donna paid the driver ('You're coughing up on the way home,' she told the Doctor). As the taxi roared away, she straightened her dress, checked her heels and nudged the Doctor, who was staring up at the night sky at the stars.

At the new star Wilf had shown him last night. Which was now brighter than before. And there seemed to be another couple of stars that he didn't think should be there...

Donna nudged him again.

'What?'

She indicated with her head towards Wilf, who was

gripping a lamppost, trying to take off his trainers and hold on to his carrier bag at the same time.

'I can't bend in this thing,' she hissed. 'If I tear it, Veena will knock me into next week. She does the whole martial arts thing.'

The Doctor took the bag from Wilf and let the old man lean on him as he slipped his trainers off and replaced them with the dress shoes.

'Sylvia bought these,' he said to the Doctor. 'Bloody things are three sizes too small.'

'No they're not,' Donna said automatically. 'You're not trying.'

'Blimey, when did you turn into your mum?' said Wilf.

Donna opened her mouth to retort, but the Doctor, sensing retreat was the better part of valour, grabbed both their arms and placed himself between them.

'Someone's dinner awaits,' he said and they marched up to the building.

The huge wooden door swung open as they reached the top step and a smartly dressed gentleman, mid-thirties, olive skin, dark hair and eyes that twinkled, waved them in.

'Good evening, Mister Mott,' he said in a slight European accent. 'Miss Noble. Doctor Smith. I am Gianni, Head of Hospitality.'

Donna pulled a 'blimey' face. 'He was well rehearsed.'

'Guest of honour,' Wilf said. 'I had to tell them who I was bringing.'

Gianni walked them into a small area where a couple of people aged somewhere between sixty and two hundred and eleventy were leaning on a bar. Or possibly the bar was holding them up. Either way, they looked like they were part of the furniture.

Donna wrinkled her nose at the strong smell of Scotch and looked behind them, where another door led to a vast dining area, and a hubbub of noise.

'Do go through,' the Head of Hospitality said, so Donna led the way.

As the trio entered the dining room, the hubbub stopped and was replaced by a round of applause led, Donna was pleased to see, by Henrietta Goodhart, resplendent in another bizarre but unusually tonally dour hat.

She walked towards them, arms outstretched, kissed Donna, then the Doctor and finally Wilf, each of them on both cheeks, Continental style. Then she planted a quick one on Wilf's lips and winked. 'I'm fine tonight,' she said to his unasked question.

A man in his late fifties walked over, and shook Wilf's hand. 'Crossland. Cedric Crossland. Doctor Cedric Crossland. Doctor Cedric Crossland CBE. But you must call me Rick, Mr Mott.'

'Oh, just Wilf'll be fine,' Wilf said, throwing a look appealing for help or rescue to Donna, the Doctor and Netty.

Donna started forward but Netty held her back. 'No, no, let him go. It's his night and he has to take the rough with the smooth, bless his cotton socks. Besides, the chocolate pudding'll make it all worthwhile.' They watched as Wilf got caught up in the celebrations. 'He looks so happy,' she said.

'I understand you have a big part to play in that,' the Doctor said, adding 'Not that I pretend to understand things like that.'

Netty grinned at him. 'Course you don't, Doctor. Being from outer space.'

The Doctor stared at her, then smiled. 'Actually, I'm from Nottingham—'

'He's from Walthamstow,' Donna said at the same time.

'Born in Nottingham,' said the Doctor.

'But brought up in Walthamstow,' added Donna, a bit sheepishly.

'Wilf told me everything, Doctor. About you. About the ATMOS stuff. About where Donna is when she's with you. No secrets, you see.'

The Doctor blew air out of his cheeks. 'Well, I'm not sure what Wilf has told you but, I'm… um… well…'

Netty touched his hand. 'It's all right. Most days I can barely remember who I am, let alone what planet you and Donna are sending postcards from. Your secret is safe with me.'

'I think I'll kill him this time,' Donna said, looking towards her grandfather who was being poured an extraordinarily large brandy by a group of old men and women.

Netty shook her head. 'He's so proud of you both, please don't be cross with him. Besides, it gives me a chance to talk to you both about the Chaos Body. You know, while I still can.'

Donna frowned.

'I'm sorry, Donna,' Netty said. 'Does me talking about

my condition embarrass you? There's no need, there's nothing I have to hide from anyone. Least of all myself.'

'It's not that,' Donna said. 'It's just… well, a bit sad.'

'It is. Very sad, believe me. But I have got used to living with it and I make the most of the lucid days because the ones that aren't are getting more and more frequent.'

'How frequent?'

'Doctor! She's not going to tell the world about us.'

But he shushed her. 'How frequent, Henrietta?'

'If I can get through to Friday remembering what I did on Tuesday, that's a victory.'

Gianni was at their side, surreptitiously as a good Head of Hospitality should be, with drinks on a silver tray for them and they grabbed the glasses quickly, as if trying to fill in a gap in the conversation.

'So,' Netty said. 'Chaos Bodies.'

'When did it show up? The first one, I mean?'

'Ah,' Netty said, 'you've noticed the others. Only saw them myself this evening and no one here tonight seems to have mentioned it.'

'That's cos they weren't there last night. Or when we left Chiswick, actually.'

Netty laughed. 'I know you know more about outer space than this lot here do put together but, scientifically, stars can't move that quickly. And if they could, the devastation would be phenomenal.'

The Doctor toasted her. 'Ah, but then they're not stars. Not real stars. The chaos bit, though, that's spot on.'

'What are they, then?' asked Donna.

The Doctor shrugged. 'I have a suspicion. The first

93

one, the original, that looks like a star certainly, and it's certainly a ball of superheated combustible energy that shares minor properties with a star, but the others, they're like satellites. But not astral ones.'

'Man-made?'

'Well, Someone-made, yes. And somewhere at the back of my head is a little voice trying to tell me where I've seen it all before.'

There was a tinkle of someone tapping a glass with a spoon.

'Ladies and gentlemen, before we eat, I should like to introduce you to our guest of honour,' Doctor Crossland was saying. 'In honour of being the first to spot the new star M7432•6, officially known as 7432MOTT, I give you – Wilfred Mott!'

There was thunderous applause and even a 'hear, hear', then one of the waiters led the Doctor, Donna and Netty to the table to join the rest of the guests.

The Doctor was nabbed by Wilf and positioned between him and Crossland, while Netty was on Wilf's other side and Donna next to her.

The Doctor looked expectantly at the empty seat to his right, wondering who was going to sit there. It was, he thought, a bit like being sat on a train and hoping the empty seat beside you isn't going to be occupied by a madman with a loud personal stereo or a kicking child or, worst of all, some frumpy businessman who would spend the whole journey loudly on his mobile phone. And, every time he hung up and someone else rang, he'd let the annoying ringtone go all the way through before answering.

The Doctor often wondered these days when these trivial little things had begun to annoy him quite so much. Must have been hitting the big 900 mark.

The seat was yanked back by a woman whose clothing could at best be described as eccentric and at worst insane, a terrible clashing of colours, styles and, well, everything. The biggest crime against fashion was the blouse she was wearing, which appeared to have Galileo's Map of the Heavens embroidered on it. By hand. They were the sort of clothes you might put on if you got dressed with both eyes closed after someone had taken your wardrobe and given it a really good shake.

Not that the wearer seemed remotely aware of her… unique haute couture. More alarmingly, none of the other members seemed to bat an eyelid either – only Wilf and especially Donna reacted, Wilf with incredulity and Donna by stifling a laugh and finding the glass of water before her suddenly the most fascinating thing on Earth.

'Ariadne Holt,' she said in a tone that suggested to the Doctor that this wasn't just an introduction but was in fact a complete explanation for why she looked as she did.

'Hullo,' he said, offering his hand. She held her own hand up as if to suggest he kiss it or, at the very least, bow slightly. He did neither, managing instead to turn it back into the handshake he had started.

She gave him a look that seemed to say, 'Oh, right, you're going to be like that are you?' and pulled her chair closer to the table and very slightly further away from him.

'So,' said Ariadne, 'What's your field?'

'Ten Acre,' he smiled.

Steely glare.

'In-joke,' he mumbled. 'Bad one.'

Steely glare again.

'I'm the Doctor, by the way.'

'I know,' Ariadne Holt said.

'You do?'

'Crossland told me. Suggested I sit. Here. Next to you. For dinner.'

'Indeed?'

'Yes.'

'Right. Well, sorry, I don't actually know Mr Crossland.'

'Doctor.'

'Yes?'

'What?'

'What?'

'He's Doctor Crossland. Not "Mister".'

'I see.'

'You're Smith. John Smith. You write books. With pictures. About the constellations, no?'

'Ah, no. Not me. Sorry. Although when I was little I used to do finger-paintings of the night sky. I used to add bits of… well, pasta you'd call it, to make the planets all 3-D. And glitter. Lots of glitter. I was very… glittery.'

Steely glare again.

'You don't really care much about my finger-paintings, do you, Ariadne? Can't say I blame you. Not much good. D-minus. Four out of ten. Harsh, but probably justified I always think. So, what do you study?'

Ariadne Holt ignored him and looked past him to Doctor Crossland. 'Wrong Smith, you old fool,' she said. 'This one's not the author.'

Crossland glanced at the Doctor. 'What is he then?'

'I'm right here,' the Doctor said.

'Ha!' snorted Donna, remembering the taxi ride.

'A fool,' Ariadne Holt replied. 'Droning on and on about finger-painting and Italian food.'

Donna gave the Doctor a double thumbs-up and an exaggerated wink.

He gave her a look that should've turned her to ice.

She grinned widely.

Crossland looked at the Doctor, then at Wilf. 'Thought you said the chappie was an expert, Mr Mott?'

Now it was Wilf's turn to look like a rabbit caught in headlights, because he was out of his comfort zone. The best he could come up with was 'He is.'

Crossland harrumphed.

'Actually,' the Doctor said, 'I think you'll find "the chappie" *is* a bit of an expert, especially on your so-called Chaos Bodies.'

That got their attention.

The Doctor took a deep breath. 'It's not a star, you know.'

'We know it isn't,' said Ariadne.

'Just don't know what it actually *is*,' Crossland said.

'I do.'

Everyone turned to look at him. 'It's lovely Ariadne that gave me the final piece of the puzzle, with that… unique blouse she's wearing.'

'Go on,' she said.

But the Doctor stopped momentarily, because he was looking at Henrietta Goodhart.

Netty was not taking part in the conversation, though no one had noticed. Instead she was staring straight ahead, like she had zoned out for a while.

Donna caught the Doctor's gaze and nodded slightly, and the Doctor gave a sad smile to her. Then he drew the attention back to himself, giving Donna time to stand Netty up, briefly resting a hand on Wilf's shoulder to stop him following. As they began to move away, the Doctor caught Donna's eye and he mouthed a 'thank you'. Then he resumed his explanation.

'It's not a star so much as a superheated ball of psionic energy which acts as a containment protective field around a malign intelligence. An intelligence that wants to dominate and expand and survive. Something it's fully entitled to do in its own little corner of space where it normally can't hurt anyone. But when it crawls out of its little dimension and enters ours, when it drags itself halfway across the universe to this planet, at this time, then I get interested. Interested and intrigued. Well, I say intrigued, I mean angry. And a bit scared. You see that Galileo star map thing reminded me of when I first encountered it, back in the fifteenth century and foolishly brought a sliver of it here, to Earth. Italy in fact. Near Florence. Well, that region. Anyway, a few slivers have found their way here now and again ever since because it's quite fascinated by Earth and this solar system.'

'You. Are. Mad.' Ariadne said quietly.

'It was the "fifteenth century" bit, wasn't it?'

Crossland was nodding. 'That. And the rest.'

Wilf tapped Crossland's arm. 'You should listen to him, Mister Doctor Crossland CBE, Sir, cos the Doctor is usually right.'

'Aww, thank you, Wilf,' the Doctor beamed.

'My pleasure, Doctor,' he replied.

'So, Doctor,' said Crossland. 'What do you call this fanciful ball of energy then?'

'Oh, that's simple,' the Doctor said. 'One word. Mandragora.'

As the Doctor said 'Mandragora', the Chaos Body began pulsating out in space. The other lights nearby pulsated in rhythmic response. And moved closer. On a mission.

As the Doctor said 'Mandragora', seven people sat bolt upright in an SUV parked in a car park at Heathrow airport, as if they'd just been switched on: the newlywed DiCottas; three students, their professor and his assistant, just arrived from Rome; and a Greek farmer, just in from Athens.

The Greek farmer was in the driver's seat. He turned the key in the ignition and switched on the lights, and the SUV began to move forward. On a mission.

As the Doctor said the word 'Mandragora', Donna Noble was sitting in the outer bar at the Royal Planetary Society with Netty, holding her hand, when she saw Gianni, the Head of Hospitality, stop pouring a drink. He opened his mouth as if about to speak. Words were being formed but no sound came out, until he gasped and finally spoke. But he spoke so softly Donna wasn't even sure he had said anything at all.

As the Doctor said the word 'Mandragora', Mr Murakami was sat in First Class on a JAL plane bound for Narita, drink in hand, eyes closed, listening to a compilation of 1960s tunes by Hibari Misora he'd downloaded onto his prototype M-TEK.

By the time he'd realised that beneath the music there were subliminal messages about MorganTech, it was too late. Something in his mind was screaming, yelling, realising exactly what the amazing ingredient was within the M-TEK, but he also knew he'd never be able to break free and warn the world.

'A drink Murakami-San?' The flight attendant offered up a choice of wine or spirits.

With a smile he opted for a glass of red wine. He tapped his earphones. 'Marvellous singer, died early. I always say it's a tragedy when so many people have to die with so much unfulfilled potential.'

With a nod, the attendant moved on to her next passenger.

Mr Murakami continued to listen to the music, his mind gradually being corrupted by all the subliminal messages being fed into it, and there was nothing he could do.

As the Doctor said the word 'Mandragora', Madam Delphi waveformed into excited life in the Penthouse Suite of the Oracle Hotel beside the Brentford Golden Mile.

'Dara Morgan,' she exclaimed. 'He is aware of me!'

Dara Morgan thought the computer would have shaken with glee if it had been possible. 'Who?'

'The Doctor. After all these aeons, after all this distance, the stars were aligned exactly as I predicted. Tomorrow's horoscopes will be very different now.'

And on Madam Delphi's website, read by people all over the world, Sunday's predictions for every sign of the Zodiac rewrote themselves.

All that they now said was 'Welcome Back! Your life will change during the next 48 hours in ways you could never imagine. Embrace this change, and prepare for the next, greatest, phase of your life as Mandragora swallows the skies, and smiles down upon you all.'

Within fifteen minutes, a man in Cape Town had put these words on a T-shirt. A woman in Paris was creating a Facebook group for Mandragora. And in Milwaukee three youths graffitied the word 'Mandragora' across the walls of their school.

The Doctor was getting exasperated with Cedric Crossland, and that other barmy woman, Ariadne something, was doing Wilf's head in, so he left them to it and took a wander back to the outer bar area.

He spotted Donna and Netty, and he knew immediately that Netty was gone, off into her own world. And Wilf's heart pounded a bit harder because, although he'd seen this a number of times, every time he did so, he asked himself a question.

What would he do if this was the last time? What if she drifted away and never came back?

Donna smiled up at him as he approached, her arm wrapped tightly around this old woman she barely knew but had taken under her wing just because her daft old granddad liked her.

Wilf pulled up a stool and sat facing them both.

'You're very good, Donna,' he said. 'You don't have to do this. She's not family.'

'Yeah, maybe not, but she's important. To you. And I reckon, deep down, to Mum as well.'

'Oh, you know your mum, always moaning, always complaining but underneath all that…'

'More moans, more complaints?' Donna roared with laughter. 'God, I love her, Gramps, but there are times I could flatten her, too.'

'Here, I'll have none of that talk, Donna. She's a good one, your mum. Speaks her mind, but that's no bad thing. And she loves you, too. She just doesn't know how to cope with a lot of things since Geoff… you know…'

'Died? You can say it.'

'Since your dad passed, yeah.'

Donna lifted her arm from Netty and reached out to take her granddad's hand in hers. 'So, how'd you meet Netty then?'

Wilf smiled. 'She wrote to me after I got a letter published in the Journal.'

'Ah, the Journal. They still going?'

'Sixty years next year. This is the International Year of Astronomy, it's all big double-sized issues. I wrote 'em a letter about the Triple Conjunction! Jupiter and Neptune! Netty saw it, disagreed with my thoughts about how difficult it'd be to see with a telescope like mine and BANG, we had a little war across about three issues. Then one day she phoned me up out of the blue, we had coffee in London to sort out our disagreements and a week later she'd used her influence to make me a member of the RPS. And here we are.'

Donna smiled at him. 'So when did you find out about her Alzheimer's?'

'Oh, she told me on our second… meeting.'

'You were gonna say "second date", weren't you? Oh, you sly old fox!' Donna stared at him. 'I'm happy for you, Gramps. To find a friend, someone you like to be with. And I reckon Mum is, too.'

'Oh, I know. She's just worried about her illness, and how much strain it puts on me. She and Netty were talking about nursing homes, but I won't have none of that.'

He looked at Henrietta Goodhart. 'She's a great lady, Donna. I wish you could see her like I do.'

'I did. At the house yesterday and this morning. She's lovely, and I think you should hang on to her.'

And Wilf felt so, so sad. 'But one day, I'm gonna lose her. It's inevitable. I looked it up on the internet.'

'Oh well, that must be true, then.'

'Seriously. It's not good. I don't mean she's going to die, but I will lose her because one day she'll retreat to wherever it is she goes and won't come back. We don't have the medicines, the knowledge to cure it. It's not fair.' Then a thought struck him. 'I bet out there, in the stars, I bet they could treat her. I bet there's something…'

And Donna squeezed his hands. 'It doesn't work like that, Gramps. God knows, with everything I've seen, all the people I've met, there've been times I thought there must be solutions to illness, famine, all sorts of nasty things. I thought if I shouted at the Doctor loud enough he could find a way. But it doesn't matter if you're in Chiswick or Cestus Minor, there are no easy answers. We just have to deal with what fate's given us.'

'It's not fair,' he repeated.

'No. No, it's not. And I'm so, so sorry for you. Because I love you, and I really like Netty and if I could find a way to make everything easy for you both, I really, really would. And you know what, the Doctor doesn't know either of you that well, but I reckon he'd try ten times harder than me. And it probably still wouldn't make a difference, so there's no point beating yourself up over something you have no control over.'

Wilf looked at Donna, and wondered what had happened to that silly, flighty girl he'd loved but worried about all those years. Now she was a fine, brave, brilliant young woman. And he loved her even more.

And then there was Netty.

He eased his hand away from Donna's and took both of Netty's in his. 'Hey you,' he said quietly. 'Henrietta Goodhart, I think it's time for a singsong, like we used to, back in the old days?'

Donna frowned in confusion, but he just winked at her. 'I know what I'm doing.'

Softly he began to hum a tune. An old gospel hymn.

'When the stars begin to fall,' he began to sing quietly, 'Oh Lord! What a morning. Oh Lord! What a morning…'

He glanced at Donna. 'She told me that her husband used to sing this with her, during the war.

'I thought she never married?'

Wilf smiled tightly. 'Never let anyone know I told you this, sweetheart. She was married. For three days. And he was killed in Singapore, when the bombing started. She told me that they'd sung this at her wedding, on the way in a big Silver Rolls. She had a photo of it and showed me, it was gorgeous. And then, when they tried to flee Singapore, he died holding her hand and she sung it to him as he lay dying in her lap.' He looked back at Netty. 'Never tell anyone I told you that, least of all her. Promise. She really loved him so much and swore she'd never marry again.'

'Course I promise, Gramps. Course I do.'

He started again. 'Oh sinner, what will you do, when the stars begin to fall... oh Lord, what a morning...'

Netty's eyes seemed to focus, and she took a deep breath, as if waking up.

'I went, didn't I? Oh no, I've not been wandering out in the streets in nothing but my underwear?' She looked at Donna and winked. 'Again!'

Wilf smiled at her, a tear almost trying to escape his eye, so he blinked it away before either of them could see it. 'I think we need to get back to the party, rescue the Doctor, yeah?'

Netty stood up and let Wilf lead the way. She hung back a little and leaned on Donna. 'I get more tired each time,' she said. 'Oh, and thank you.'

'For what?'

'His name was Richard Philip Goodhart. And your grandfather is the only person I've ever met who comes close.'

By the time they'd made their way back to the main hall, the dinner was over.

Wilf and the Doctor were now propping up the far wall, and Wilf was apologising because Ariadne Holt and Cedric Crossland had refused to take the Doctor seriously. 'I'm embarrassed to know them.'

The Doctor looked at Wilf in sadness. 'Don't be. These are good people. Some of them are a bit odd, but at heart they're just marvellously normal. Why should they believe me?'

'Well, we have had spaceships and Sontarans and stuff over the last few years.'

'There's no accounting for mankind's ability to rationalise things, Wilf. What one group of people will be scared by, another group see no danger from because it's within their comfort zone. These people are marvellous pioneers, loving the stars, the constellations and just watching and noting and cataloguing the heavens. Like you! None of that should ever stop, it's too important, even if things are unlikely to be recognised for a couple of centuries. Nobody took Galileo or Copernicus or Organon seriously in their own times.'

'You take their rudeness very well, Doctor.'

The Doctor shrugged. 'It's not personal. People like Doctor Crossland just don't want to contemplate things that fall outside their sphere of reference. At worst its foolhardy, at best easily overlooked.' Then he looked at the glass of lemonade in his hand. 'Usually.'

'But this Mandragora stuff, that's not usual, is it?'

The Doctor shook his head. 'It's a malevolent entity, Wilf. Last time it was here in force, a lot of people died.

But it was trying to stop the Italian Renaissance, to stop science reaching the state it's at now. I can't see what it hopes to achieve today. Go back forty years and stop the transistor, or the microchip and yes, you'd spoil the next generation of human progress. But here? Nothing particularly special happens this year, this decade even, that can really affect Earth's future that much. You lot just plod on for a century or so. Getting out to Mars. A couple of major space flights—'

'Mars? We get to Mars? Do we find Martians?'

'Spoilers,' the Doctor winked. 'My lips are sealed.' He swigged his lemonade. 'So I'm not sure whether to leave the Mandragora Helix alone up there and assume that it's just keeping an eye on things, or be prepared for a big battle.'

'Perhaps it's got something to do with those Carnes boys, Doctor. You said you thought they had aliens in the family.'

'Oh yes! And how did Joe Carnes know my name?' The Doctor sighed. 'Oh Wilf, Wilf, Wilf! You just ruined a perfectly pleasant evening.'

'I did? How? And, um, sorry.'

'Because you just spotted a chink, a tiny, tiny flaw in my logic. Mandragora is linked, in a bizarre way, to astrology, not just astronomy.'

'Astrology's nonsense.'

'Well, most of it's just made up by newspapers. But it dates back to the Dark Times, so there's probably *something* in it. Go back to the birth of the universe and you'll see every society, every civilisation has some form of zodiac, a belief in the power of ancient lights linked to some kind of belief system based around the movement of planets and stars and constellational shift. Astrologers on the planet Hynass swear blind that there's no such thing as coincidence and have absolute faith in the knowledge that every event since the Big Bang has been divined, is a matter of pre-established fate that no one can ever break out of. Now you might think it's nonsense and I might think it's nonsense, but Mandragora thrives on that belief, that unproven system, and uses it. Cause and effect.'

Wilf frowned. 'But it's still nonsense.'

'Oh yes! Yeah, course it is. Nonsense! Well, probably. Doesn't stop Mandragora being able to tap into those energies, though.'

Wilf shrugged. 'Whatever you say, Doctor.'

Donna walked over. 'Granddad, I think Netty could do with some support against that mad old witch's opinions on a woman's place in modern society.'

Wilf nodded. 'Cheers, Doctor. I hope you're wrong by the way.' And he wandered off.

'What was that all about then, sunshine? You upsetting my gramps?'

The Doctor shook his head. 'No, Donna, not at all. He's got me thinking about coincidence and causality.' He glanced over at Netty. 'How is she?'

'Not sure. She just drifted off for a while but then she just seemed to wake up, all smiles and dragged me back here.'

'It happens, I'm afraid,' he said, still observing her as she slipped an arm around Wilf's waist. 'And don't forget, she's used to it herself.'

Donna tapped his hand. 'And there's something else. In the bar. That good-looking bloke who showed us in earlier?'

'Gianni?'

'Yeah, him. He was going on about someone.'

'Who?'

'Dunno, I wasn't sure he was even speaking at first but it seemed to be something about a man licking a mad dolphin.'

The Doctor shrugged. 'Could be anything. Probably had too much to drink himself.'

'Or working with these people has sent him nutty,' Donna grinned. 'Oh well. Not sure why you'd lick a mad dolphin, though.'

The Doctor laughed. 'Nor me. We should think of heading off soon, though.'

'Why?'

'Something to do with a very old and dangerous alien entity suspended not far above your planet that is unlikely to be there sightseeing.'

'How dangerous?'

'Well, it'll be waiting for something like a lunar eclipse which, looking at the moon tonight, doesn't seem especially imminent.'

'There's always the Triple Conjunction.'

'The what?'

'Gramps told me about it, it's why they're all so excited by his discovery of that new star. This is the International Year of Astronomy, and they're all waiting to see the first triple conjunction between Jupiter and Neptune.'

Donna was quite proud that she'd retained all that information, but the Doctor was legging it across the room to Doctor Crossland. 'The Triple Conjunction,' he yelled. 'When is it?'

'Sorry?'

'This year, yes? But when this year?'

Crossland sighed. 'I thought you were supposed to be clever?'

'I am. But, like all clever people, I can only learn things when people give me straight answers to straight questions and not sarcasm.'

Doctor Crossland looked triumphant. He had outsmarted the Doctor. 'Well, if you knew as much about astronomy as you say, you'd know it's ongoing. It started a while back.'

'When the Chaos Body was first sighted?'

'I suppose so, yes.'

'And when does it hit its peak?'

'It's why we're having this dinner, Doctor. The main event occurs on Monday, about three o'clock in the afternoon, local time.'

'You appear to be looking very smug, Doctor Crossland,' the Doctor said, 'for a man who may well be dead in forty-eight hours. Give or take five or six hours.'

Doctor Crossland frowned. 'Is that a threat?'

'Yes,' the Doctor said. 'Not from me, from me it's an assurance. The threat is from Mandragora. From your Chaos Body. It's here to kill you all.'

He hurried over to Wilf, Netty and Ariadne Holt. 'Sorry to break up the party, Wilf, but I have to go. Can you get Netty home OK, Donna?'

'Oh, Doctor, you go, don't worry about us. I have a cab booked to take me home at eleven anyway,' Netty said. She touched Wilf's arm. 'And don't even try to argue with me, Wilfred Mott. This is your night, so I didn't want you feeling all responsible for me tonight.'

Wilf looked from her to the Doctor.

'Wilf can't leave,' said Ariadne Holt. 'We haven't done the presentation yet.'

'It's only us that's going,' said Donna. 'Granddad will stay.'

'Like hell I will,' said Wilf. 'I'm coming with you.'

'No one's coming with me,' the Doctor said, but no one was listening to him.

Donna pulled him closer. 'Gramps, Netty has already had one... spell this evening. You have to stay with her. Make sure she gets home. Go with her in the cab, then keep the cab and get home, yeah?' She reached into her handbag and took out three tenners. 'Dunno if it's enough, but it should help.'

Wilf refused the money. 'I can pay my own way, thank you, sweetheart.'

'Yes, I'm sure you can,' Donna said. 'But take it anyway, so I don't have it on my conscience that you might've got stranded somewhere and have to drag Mum out of bed to come and pick you up, all right?'

Wilf looked at his granddaughter, then at the Doctor, who pretended to find something interesting on the ceiling. He took the cash. 'Call me,' he said. 'I've got my mobile.'

'I know you have. And it'll be switched off or have a flat battery. Same as always. We'll be fine, I'll see you in the morning.' She kissed him, then Netty and grabbed the Doctor's hand. 'Come on you, time we were gone.'

The Doctor called goodbye to Netty, Wilf and Ariadne Holt as Donna dragged him through the door and back into the entranceway, past the doorman and out into the cold night air. 'I was going by myself,' he protested, but Donna had already waved down a cab (well, stood in the middle of South Lambeth Road and whistled down one that had made the right choice between stopping, ignoring her or running her over).

Donna clambered in, hauling the Doctor in afterwards.

'Where to?' asked the cabbie. 'I'm off duty soon, so better not be far.'

'Chiswick High Road,' the Doctor said to him, adding to Donna, 'I need the TARDIS.'

The driver pulled out, drove under the railway bridge and headed back towards Nine Elms and West London.

The first report came in at 23.04. It was from the Clemenstry Observatory in Western Australia. It reported that the new star, the one that had appeared in the heavens a week or so back, seemed to be moving in conjunction with another star, M84628•7.

Which was a bit unusual, Professor Melville declared, jabbing at his computer screen with a ballpoint pen. He was in his office at the Copernicus Array in Essex, but probably wanted to be in the radio telescope control room itself. He usually did.

'That's the problem with these new stars, these Chaos Bodies,' he said to his young 'assistant', Miss Oladini.

'They're chaotic and make no sense, scientifically speaking. Don't you agree?'

'On the nose, Professor,' she said, not having a clue what he was talking about. She was only here on a short-term contract from the Lovelace Agency in Brentwood, finding temporary work placements to learn new skills. 'New skills' – she was 25 and already needed 'new skills'. Somewhat embarrassingly, she wasn't remotely interested in astronomy but didn't have the heart to tell Melville that. Instead, she kept him fed and watered with chocolate bars and tea and listened to him talk about his cat and his mother. (He lived with one and was talking about having the other put to sleep as it had bad kidneys, but Miss Oladini still wasn't entirely sure which way round it was. She had a sneaking suspicion, however, the cat was the healthy one.)

Professor Melville was a sweet old man. Emphasis on the 'sweet'. And the 'old'. He said he'd been a pop star back in the Sixties, but she wasn't sure she believed him. Miss Oladini certainly liked him, though she rather suspected he was only employed at the Copernicus Array (cos surely he was way beyond retirement age) out of sympathy. Probably why he took the night shifts, keep him out of trouble.

The Copernicus Array itself was a radio telescope built in the gardens of an old Georgian mansion house that had been converted into the Array's offices, meeting rooms and so on. A shame, Miss Oladini thought. It was a lovely old house – she often liked visiting old houses and although a lot of care had been taken to preserve the original fixtures and fittings, this place seemed sterile and lacking in natural character. She often wondered who had lived here hundreds of years back, what had become of them all and how they'd feel about their drawing rooms, kitchens, bedrooms and ballrooms being converted into rooms full of dull scientists and administrators.

At 23.09, the report had come in from the Griffin Observatory in Maryland. It too mentioned the Chaos Body moving into alignment with another star. But a different one to Clemenstry's M84628•7. This was M97658•3. Which was patently absurd.

'Have they all been drinking?' Melville wondered.

That seemed like quite a good idea to Miss Oladini, though she only really wanted to get home to her bed. She wasn't keen on cycling in the dark and, at this time of night, there were lots of people on the roads who might be a bit worse for wear.

At 23.17, the report came in from the Tycho Project, near Beaconsfield. The Chaos Body was edging towards M29034•1.

Of course, this wasn't all simultaneous – after all, it wasn't dark in California or Perth right now, it was just that Melville was doing a night shift and had only just turned his computer on.

'All we need now, Miss Oladini, is Minsk to offer us something daft and—'

And sure enough, at 23.19, the Colossus in Minsk fed through details of how the Chaos Body was in alignment with M23116•3.

Now Melville was alert and curious. Miss Oladini, too, despite her lack of interest in astronomy, because she'd been a mathematics student (hence her ending up here) and she calculated the odds of one Chaos Body suddenly forming a new constellation with four pre-existing stars all on the same night to be… well, bigger odds than there were numerical spaces on her calculator.

Melville patched through the latest photos onto the big screen that dominated one wall of his office. It was indeed a big screen, and state-of-the-art technology that other observatories and radio telescopes around the UK would have donated a lot of right arms for. All Melville had to do was trace an invisible line from his laptop screen to the big screen on the wall and images and words flowed from one to the other like something out of a sci-fi movie. Melville was proud of the software, but hadn't a clue how it worked. He just knew it did and it meant he could move images around on the wall-sized screen without leaving his chair. Which he was doing now.

First he centred his own photo of the Chaos Star. Then he overlayed Clemenstry's. Then Griffin's, Tycho's and finally Colossus's.

'Professor…?'

'I know.'

'But that's…'

'I know.'

'I mean, how…'

'I don't know.'

'I've never seen anything like it.'

'I know.'

Melville grabbed a phone on his desk. It was red. As

he started punching in numbers, he glanced up at Miss Oladini. 'Have you signed the OSA, Miss Oladini?'

She frowned. 'Do what?'

'The Official Secrets Act. Did they make you sign it when you got your work placement forms for this place at the agency?'

Miss Oladini thought for a moment. Melville was scaring her with the question. Normally, he was a nice old guy, bit dotty, bit rambling, smoked his pipe too often. But now he was suddenly alert and officious, stern and all sense of 'eccentric' gone.

And Miss Oladini realised that the silly, fussy, dotty old man was an act. Underneath it all, Professor Melville was sharp as a whistle. Maybe he really had been a pop singer.

'Well?'

She nodded. She had signed something that had the word 'official' in it, she remembered that. Frankly she hadn't taken much notice of it when Mrs Lovelace at the agency had got her to sign. All the temps signed bits of paper for health and safety, insurance waivers that sort of thing, when they got their placements. One extra hadn't meant much at the time.

Now it seemed big and scary.

'Why?'

'Because without your signature on the bottom of that form, what I'm about to do and what you're about to hear would have us both in jail for the rest of our lives if you haven't.'

And Miss Oladini thought hard. Her brain was good with numbers. 'Form KD62344,' she said suddenly. 'I signed it twice and initialled a box, bottom left.'

Melville winked. 'Thank you.' He punched a final number on the phone. 'Aubrey Fairchild, please. This is the Copernicus Array, Code 18. My name is Melville.'

Miss Oladini looked back at the assembled collage of images. The Chaos Body plus the other stars on display meant nothing individually. But now that Melville had put them together, they formed a picture. And not just some abstract nonsense that people saw as a couple of fish, or a plough or a rollercoaster.

This was very clearly, distinctly and sharply a face. A face with a mouth twisted into a laugh.

Miss Oladini shivered because that laugh wasn't a happy laugh. It was pure malevolence.

'Prime Minister? Melville, Administrative Professor at the Copernicus Array. I'm sending you a Code 18 image.' There was a pause. 'Yes, sir. No, sir, the images have only been combined here, it's still a UK threat but give it a few hours…'

Professor Melville looked across at Miss Oladini. 'No, sir, just myself and my assistant. We'll stay put until we hear from your people, Prime Minister. No, absolutely, total lockdown, no communications in or out of the Copernicus Array under any circumstances. Goodnight, sir.'

Professor Melville replaced the phone.

'That was really the Prime Minister?' Miss Oladini asked.

Melville nodded. 'I'm sorry, my dear, but I think we're in for a long night here. Could you check where we are regarding tea and milk?'

Miss Oladini started to leave the room, then turned back to see Melville take a mobile phone from his jacket pocket. She hadn't even known he had a mobile phone. 'Professor? Didn't you just promise Mr Fairchild that we'd have no communications?'

He smiled. 'That's why I need you to check on the tea. If you are not in the room, you can't be held responsible when I break that promise, commit treason and quite probably professional suicide. Now, for your sake, off you go.'

Confused, Miss Oladini left the office. But she waited just outside the door, to see if she could hear who he was calling.

She heard the tell-tale electronic beeps of the keypad then, after what must have been quite a few rings, he spoke. 'Good evening, my name is Professor Melville. May I speak with the Doctor, please?'

The cab was about halfway down Prince Albert Drive, between Vauxhall and Chiswick, doing nearly 20 because of the speed humps.

In the back of the cab, Donna took out her ringing phone and stared at the number, but didn't recognise it. With a shrug, she pressed accept. 'Hallo?'

She listened and then passed it over to the Doctor.

He smiled. 'I had the TARDIS routed to your number. Should've told you. Sorry.'

'How did you cope before mobiles?' she sighed. 'A Professor Melville, apparently.'

The Doctor grinned. 'And there's another coincidence – it's one of those nights, isn't it,' he said before speaking into the phone. 'Ahab! What can I do for the Copernicus Array tonight? As if I can't guess. Does it involve the phrase Chaos Body?'

Miss Oladini was having her fill of surprising things tonight. First the stars making pictures. Then dotty old Professor Melville having hotlines to the Prime Minister. Then discovering that the milk in the kitchenette hadn't gone off for once. Oh, and then her boyfriend phoning at nearly midnight.

'Spencer? What do you want?'

'Don't tell me you haven't used that bloody great telescope to look at the sky?'

Miss Oladini crossed to the kitchen door, the one that led outside, not into the corridor and peeked out into the cold night air, not really thinking she'd see anything with the naked eye.

So she was quite surprised when she could.

'Is it some kind of firework display?' Spencer asked.

She wondered what to say. Ten minutes earlier, the skies had been clear and the laughing face could only be seen in photographs. Now it was very visible across the heavens, and if her daft old boyfriend had spotted it – and not written it off as a lager-fuelled trip – then something needed to be done. She remembered the Official Secrets Act and told Spencer that yes, it was probably just something being projected from the roof of one of the cinemas down Dagenham way. 'A movie promotional thing,' she said, adding 'and they phoned and warned us about it yesterday,' which was an awful lie, but seemed to make Spencer happy.

After he'd rung off, it crossed her mind that the rest of Britain might not be quite so ready to believe her story – not least because she couldn't phone each person individually and tell them.

Maybe the Prime Minister would. Or Patrick Moore.

'How's the tea coming?'

Miss Oladini turned to see Melville in the doorway, a big smile on his face. She mentioned that the face from the photo was now visible in the sky, and Melville wandered over to the window and peered through.

'Not to worry,' he said. 'An expert's looking into it.'

'From Downing Street?'

'Oh no. Someone far better equipped than anyone there.' He glanced out of the window. 'Horrible-looking thing, isn't it?' he said, as the kettle began to boil again. 'Milk no sugar wasn't it, Miss Oladini?'

She nodded mutely.

'I'm not worried now,' he added. 'The Doctor will sort it all out.'

There was a flash of lights from outside, and they heard a couple of cars pull up in the staff car park.

'That was quick,' Melville muttered, frowning slightly.

'Downing Street or your Doctor friend?' she asked, trying not to sound nervous. 'Or maybe someone else from round here, concerned by the thing in the sky?'

But Melville wasn't listening, really. He was watching to see who was in the cars.

The headlights were left full on, beaming in through the kitchenette window, so they couldn't see who got out of the car, just heard the sounds of doors opening and slamming.

Miss Oladini shivered. This felt… wrong.

Melville presumably agreed, because he suddenly dashed for the outside door, as if to bolt it. He was too late. Someone shoved the door open.

Melville stood in front of Miss Oladini, chivalrously protecting her from whoever the newcomers were.

There were… well, a lot of them, different ages, not looking especially… government-ish. Or terribly threatening.

But there was something about them, Miss Oladini thought, something about the way they looked around the kitchenette, their heads moving unnaturally as if they were seeing the inside of a kitchen for the first time.

An old, fat man was at the front, a middle-aged man behind him. Behind them were an old woman and a trio of student-types, two men and a woman.

'Where are the others?' the first old man asked in an American accent.

Professor Melville cleared his throat. 'This is private property. This is the Copernicus Array. You can't just turn up at gone midnight and—'

The young student woman pushed past the others, looking at Melville as if she couldn't quite understand why he was standing there. 'You… work here?' she said.

English, that one.

He nodded. 'I am in charge of the radio telescope, and this evening I am in charge of the whole project. I should warn you that you have tripped an alarm and the police will be here in minutes.'

Another student spoke. His voice sounded European, Spanish or maybe Italian. 'I cannot detect any such alarm system. The human is lying.'

Human? What a strange expression.

But Professor Melville seemed unfazed by the choice of words, indeed, he almost relished them. 'What planet do you represent? Are you connected with that Chaos constellation?'

The large American spoke again. 'You may be of use to us.'

Without missing a beat, Melville pointed to Miss Oladini. 'And my assistant. If you need my help, you'll need hers, too. Everything at Copernicus requires two experienced operators.'

Was he mad, Miss Oladini wondered.

'She's a highly qualified physicist and is an expert in the field of the cosmic sciences.'

Definitely mad.

'Something is wrong here,' said the older woman, also an American, walking forward. Without warning, she reached out and touched Professor Melville's shoulder. At first Miss Oladini assumed they'd both been electrocuted as a fierce purplish spark shot between them, and Melville staggered slightly, gasping in pain.

'Professor?' Miss Oladini found her voice, but immediately regretted it.

Melville turned to look at her and, for a second, she could still see vestiges of that purple light in his eyes. 'All right, I lied. She's my temporary assistant,' Melville said breathlessly. 'She has no understanding of the Copernicus Array and is harmless.'

'We can absorb her.'

'Let her go, please…'

Melville collapsed, and the three students stepped over him as they headed towards her.

Miss Oladini did the one thing no amount of chats with Mrs Lovelace in Brentwood, or Health and Safety forms or 100 words per minute could have prepared her for. She spun round and ran for her life, clattering out of the kitchenette and back into the heart of the corridors and offices of the Copernicus Array. Somehow she knew she was running for her life.

The cab was driving along past the Earls Court Exhibition Centre when the Doctor tapped on the glass and asked the driver, 'Can you pull over for just one minute, please.'

'Well?' Donna asked the Doctor, as the cab slowed down.

'Ummm, well… Actually you need to head home, because I'm going to ask this nice man to drive me somewhere else.'

'Chiswick High Road?'

The Doctor frowned, then remembered where the TARDIS was parked. 'No. No actually, bit further than that.'

Donna realised. 'You're going to see matey boy on the phone, at that telescope place. Copper Knickers or whatever it was called.'

'Where to then, mate?' the exasperated taxi driver asked.

'Essex. Just off the A127.'

The driver snorted. 'At this time of night? I live in Bounds Green. I told you I was off home.'

'Then it won't take you as long to get home from there, will it "mate",' Donna snapped. 'How much will it cost? Cos I guarantee the Doctor's not got much cash on him. And as I already subbed Granddad tonight, I might as well do him too.'

'One hundred.'

'OK,' the Doctor said.

'OK?' squawked Donna. 'How is a hundred quid "OK"?'

The Doctor ignored her and leaned towards the driver. 'But I need to get there a bit quick.'

'Hundred and twenty, then.'

'Whatever,' the Doctor sighed. 'Donna, I'll see you tomorrow. You can get another cab home from here, yes? Oh, and Donna?'

'Yes?'

'You got that hundred and twenty pounds on you?'

Donna looked like she was going to clobber him, then spoke to the driver. 'Essex,' she snapped. 'Via a cashpoint, please.'

The Doctor raised an eyebrow. 'Donna?'

'Sunshine,' Donna grinned. 'If I'm giving you a hundred plus to go to a snazzy radio telescope, I'm coming along for the ride.'

The Doctor beamed. 'Hoped you'd say that.'

And the taxi drove up towards Kensington as the Doctor and Donna made plans.

Wilf and Netty were saying their farewells, apologising for bringing the night to a premature end.

'We'll do this again soon,' Ariadne Holt told them.

'And have the actual presentation.'

'I'm so sorry to have to dash off,' Wilf lied, 'but something has come up. I need to see Miss Goodhart home. Please forgive me.'

'Nothing to forgive,' Crossland said, slapping his back. 'Any excuse for a dinner party, eh? Next week's meeting?'

On his face, Wilf had a fixed smile, but his eyes told a different story. 'I'd really enjoy that,' he said.

Netty leaned in and whispered to him. 'They'll be all right. The Doctor knows what he's doing.'

Wilf smiled at her, trying to look more reassured than he actually felt.

He wondered if he should have gone with them.

And he wondered more what Sylvia was going to say when he turned up just after midnight without them.

The Copernicus Array was in darkness when the cab pulled up in the public car park. Donna paid the grumpy driver, who headed Londonwards as quickly as possible.

'Can I just ask how we get home from here?' she hissed to the Doctor as they snuck about in the darkness. 'It's a long way back.'

'Walk?'

Donna poked his shoulder, and as he looked at her, she motioned downwards, implying he should look at her clothing.

'You look lovely,' he smiled, putting his brainy specs on.

'Well thank you, Casanova, but that wasn't my point. I am dolled up to the eyeballs in a party frock that isn't designed to be worn on a forty-mile trek across England.' She sighed. 'I had to borrow this, you know. Veena's not going to forgive me if it gets damaged. And if she doesn't forgive me, God knows what she'll do to you when I tell her who it was that made me walk all that way in it.'

'Don't tell her, then.'

Donna gave up and tried a new tack. 'OK, so why are we here and why are the lights off? Surely, if it's an observatory and it's night time, this place should be at the height of its working day?'

'Good point, well observed. And that's why we're crawling around in the car park and bushes and not marching up to the front door.'

'But I thought your mate worked here.'

'He does.'

'So why aren't we marching up to the front door and saying, "Hello, mate of the Doctor's, you called, we came"?'

The Doctor was staring at a car parked across the lawn in the staff car park. 'What's wrong with that car?'

Donna peered through the gloom. 'They don't know how to park straight?'

'And?'

'They'll ruin the grass?'

'And?'

'And... the lights are dying?'

'That's the one.'

'So?'

The Doctor grinned. 'Think about it. How old does that car look?'

'New. So it should've beeped to tell them they'd left their lights on. So they ignored it. And if it's that new, the thingy wotsit that makes the lights work shouldn't lose power so soon. Dad left the lights on overnight a couple of years ago and they were still on the next morning and the car was fine. And his car was ancient.'

The Doctor walked towards the car, sonic screwdriver in hand, and scanned the vehicle. 'Huge energy drain, locally,' he muttered.

Donna tapped his arm. 'Hey, you seen that?'

The Doctor followed her view. Up in the sky was a grinning face made of stars. 'City glow must've hidden that on the drive out here,' he said quietly.

'Fireworks?'

'Let's hope most people think so,' he replied.

'Not fireworks, then.'

'Not fireworks,' he confirmed. 'A Chaos Body at work.'

'What's a Chaos Body when it's at home?'

The Doctor shrugged. 'No idea. Your granddad introduced me to the concept last night. But a new star that can draw other stars across the sky into an alignment like that? Pretty chaotic I'd say.'

'Me too.' Donna wandered up to the front door of the Copernicus Array building. 'Well, we're not gonna learn much out here, are we?' She found a number of bells and rang the one that said EMERGENCY ONLY.

Nothing happened.

'Local energy drain, I'd guess.' Donna smiled at him.

The Doctor sighed and caught up with her, zapping the door with the sonic and pushing it open.

127

Total darkness.

'So, who's this Professor matey of yours, then?'

The Doctor was using the blue glow of the sonic as a torch, trying to identify office nameplates. 'Met him years ago. One of a number of people on this planet who I can turn to from time to time if I need specialist help. And they can call me if they need me, vice versa.' He pointed upwards. 'Professor Melville's office is one floor up, the array's control room is out the back, across the gardens and turn left.'

'Dull office or exciting telescope?'

The Doctor grinned, looking slightly spooky in the blue light of his sonic. 'Are you trying to influence my choices, Donna Noble?'

'Course telescope not, Doctor. I wouldn't telescope dream of trying to telescope tell you what to do or where to go.'

The Doctor gave her a look at the last comment, and she laughed. 'Well, all right,' she said, 'but not in that sense.'

'For some reason, I think we should investigate the telescope.'

'It's like Derren Brown's in this very room,' Donna laughed.

They followed the corridor from the front door till they reached a set of French windows leading out to a patio. The Doctor sonicked them open, and they went back out into the cool night air.

'We're being watched,' Donna said after they'd been walking for a couple of minutes.

'How do you know?'

'My hair is curling,' she replied. 'That and the fact that I can see them ahead of us.'

The Doctor peered further into the gloom.

There was a group of men and women standing by the entrance to the Array itself.

Donna looked up at the cold metal structure of steps and walkways leading to a cabin that was dominated by the bowl-shaped radar dish that made up the Array.

'I'm impressed,' she said.

'By them?'

'No, by the Array. Never seen a radio telescope before, except on the telly. Nice.' She suddenly called out to the group. 'Nice dish you've got, thanks for letting us come and view it. Is there a gift shop? Love to buy my granddad a mug with a picture on it. Or a fridge magnet.'

'Or,' the Doctor joined in, 'a tea towel. Do you do tea towels? Everyone does tea towels these days. Never been sure why you'd buy a tea towel of somewhere, but there you go.'

No response from the group.

'I'm actually looking for a Professor Melville,' the Doctor continued. 'Is he here? Is he all right?'

A small man with a scar on his cheek stepped forward.

'Is that him?' Donna whispered.

The Doctor shook his head. 'Nope. Shame.'

'Excellent,' the man intoned, a slight accent marring his otherwise precise English. 'You are the Doctor.'

'What makes you say that?'

'We can sense that you are not… entirely human.'

'"Entirely"?' The Doctor seemed affronted. 'I'm not

remotely human, thank you. Dreadful species. Always fighting and grumbling.'

'Oi!' said Donna.

'See what I mean? Barely raised themselves above the use of guttural noises and, blimey, that stuff they call pop music. I mean, I know I'm getting on a bit, but it comes to something when you really can't tell the boys from the girls or understand the lyrics, doesn't it? Then of course there's the food. Have you ever had one of their hamburgers?'

The older man raised his hand to stop the Doctor's gabbling, so he did, but smiled. 'I could go on all night, but I'm guessing that might annoy you, so what do you say we just chat instead about why you've taken over these poor people's minds?'

'It's lineage,' the little man replied.

The Doctor threw a look to Donna, and she could see that wasn't an answer he'd been expecting. 'As in genealogy?' he called back.

'Four of the humans here can trace their families back to one specific place in time. That gives me power over them.'

'And the others?'

'Drones. Slaves. Willing servants.'

'Willing? Really? That's nice. Not really true, though, is it? But if you want to believe it, fair enough.' The Doctor started walking towards them, so Donna had to follow. 'OK then, where are you from originally?' He pointed up to the face formation in the skies. 'Something to do with that, I'm guessing.'

The small man with the scar shrugged. 'All in good

time, Doctor. Madam Delphi needs to speak with you.'

He raised his arm in the Doctor's direction and, before Donna could so much as gasp, a thick, crackling blast of purplish-red light shot out from his fingertips, smacking the Doctor straight in the chest and knocking his body back a couple of feet.

He was almost unconscious by the time Donna reached him. 'Get away… warn people…' was all he managed before his eyes rolled back and the rhythmic rising and falling of his burned chest slowed to an unconscious crawl.

Donna knew there was nothing she could do right away other than what he'd asked of her. She had to find help.

'And the human?' asked one of the others in the group.

'Kill her,' the man replied, and Donna saw the others all raise their arms in similar gestures.

'Not today, thank you,' Donna yelled and ran back towards the French windows, zigzagging as she ran, aware of bolts of purple energy crashing into the trees on either side of her.

She was almost at the French windows when they exploded into metal and glass around her.

Throwing her arms over her face, Donna ran straight through the debris and into the darkened mansion. She made her way into a hallway, where a huge wooden staircase went to the upper levels.

'Seen the movies,' she muttered. She headed to the rear of the steps where, sure enough, there was a doorway leading to a cellar.

She wrenched it open, counted to three and slammed it shut, really loudly.

She then tiptoed to one of the offices and slipped inside it.

Seconds later, alerted by her ruse, a small group of the people from outside arrived at the cellar door. She watched as two of them walked down the steps, leaving one on guard. Damn, she had hoped they'd all go down and she could shut them in down there.

The one on guard seemed to be looking around and for a second Donna thought he'd work out where she was hiding. Then another person she'd not seen before suddenly crashed into the man, sending him flying heavily into a wall.

The newcomer rammed a chair against the door handle of the cellar, trapping the two inside as Donna had planned and then yelled straight at her: 'Come on!'

Donna ran straight to her new ally and allowed herself to be led down a corridor.

'Kitchen…' the newcomer breathed. 'This way…'

There was a small explosion and Donna guessed the duo had blasted their way out of the cellar. 'Good idea while it lasted,' she grinned. 'I'm Donna Noble.'

'I'm Miss Oladini,' said Miss Oladini hurriedly. 'Nice to meet you. Car?'

'Came by cab.'

'No, *their* car?'

'Worth a try.'

They crashed through the kitchenette door and into the staff car park, straight towards the abandoned car. Donna took the driving seat.

'Keys?' asked Miss Oladini.

'No keys,' Donna said. 'Cos life's never that convenient.'

Miss Oladini reached down under the dashboard and yanked out some wires. 'Misspent youth,' she said.

The engine turned over sluggishly, and then died again.

'Once more,' Donna urged. 'But if it doesn't work, give up, cos they'll know where we are by now!'

Miss Oladini tried the hotwiring again, with no luck.

Two of their pursuers appeared at the kitchen door, arms raised.

'Run!' Donna screamed and threw herself out and away from the car as the purple energy smashed into it and the car exploded.

Donna was lying in some bushes, Veena's dress in tatters. 'Oh, I am so dead,' she muttered.

There was no sign of Miss Oladini, but it was difficult to see anything with the burning car blotting out her view. Donna looked around and saw a bicycle propped up against a far wall.

'You have got to be kidding me,' she muttered, then looked at her clothes. 'Nothing ventured, nothing gained.'

Hoping the same flames that were hiding her attackers from her would keep her out of their point of view, she slipped across the lawn to the bike.

With one last look around for Miss Oladini, and a sad realisation that the car had most likely become her funeral pyre, Donna grabbed the bike and clambered onto it. She wobbled slightly, slowly getting used to riding again, and then shot off down the pathway and then onto the main road.

No way was she going to get back to Chiswick by bike, she didn't have three days spare, but it might get her to the nearest town.

As Donna pedalled furiously, the burning car lit up the front of the Copernicus Array behind her, flames reflecting off the mansion's huge windows. But of people she could see no sign.

SUNDAY

When she was growing up, Donna had heard the phrase 'the shot that was heard around the world' used to describe the effect the assassination of US President John Kennedy had on the whole of western civilisation. People always said they could remember where they were when it happened.

As a child of the 1970s, she grew up hearing about things like the moon landing, the murders of both Kennedys and Martin Luther King, and Winston Churchill's state funeral, but never wholly understood them. In a childhood of spacehoppers, Donny Osmond, chopper bikes and Green Shield Stamps, words like 'Blitz' and 'rationing' and 'bubble and squeak' just meant the old people were reminiscing about twenty years previously and probably moaning that the youth of today never knew when they had it so good.

The first time Donna had found herself saying that – to one of the neighbourhood kids who'd scratched her late father's car – she was appalled at herself. She had finally become exactly what she'd derided in her parents and grandparents when she was their age. Nowadays there was nothing she liked to hear more than Granddad Wilf go on about the war, his life in the parachute regiment or Nanna Eileen's days as a Land Girl.

Today was a day like 22 November 1963 – a day when another shot would be heard around the world.

Sunday had, to be honest, started pretty badly. Donna had woken in her bed (this was a good thing), although she'd only had about two hours' sleep (this was a bad thing).

Veena's tattered dress was chucked on the floor (bad thing); next to it, a receipt she had got from the minicab driver (bad thing – who was she gonna claim that back from?) who had driven her from somewhere called South Woodham Ferrers back to Chiswick. The receipt was for £225 (very, very bad – her account had to be empty by now). Wilf had been awake when she got back in (very good thing) and had listened as she told him everything that had happened at the Copernicus Array. He had held her tight, promised that they'd find a way to rescue the Doctor and sent her to sleep it all off.

Donna had been furious with herself – she'd left the Doctor there, she'd abandoned him in a way he'd never do to her (bad thing). But she was also practical. He'd told her to go, and that had been right because otherwise she'd have been killed (definitely a bad thing).

Donna felt like death but needed to get help and go back to the Array.

Perhaps she could track down Martha Jones and her mates at UNIT – she liked Martha and knew she'd drop everything to help.

As she reached the bottom of the stairs, she picked up the Yellow Pages and was already halfway to U when she realised that UNIT was unlikely to be there, filed under Military Organisations Dedicated to Wiping Out Martians (neither good nor bad, just a bit trigger-happy).

'Well good morning, madam,' Sylvia Noble snapped across the hallway. 'I was worried about you last night.'

'Why?'

'Oh, I don't know. Crawling back in at the crack of dawn after a night clubbing with the Doctor? At your age? I mean, clubbing's great when you're 21, but when middle age is only a few birthdays away—'

'Oi!'

'Whatever. Point is, it's time to grow up, young lady.'

'Thanks, Mum. Too old to go clubbing, not too old to live with my mother. Great.'

'No one forces you to live here,' Sylvia said, putting a cup of tea in Donna's hands. 'Not that you do much these days. Off with Daddy Longlegs for weeks on end.' Sylvia tugged at Donna's dressing gown, tightening the belt, straightening out the collar. 'And where's he today, then? Dragged your granddad off up the allotment, no doubt. And it's not a warm morning, and he's left his thermos here.' Sylvia licked her forefinger and de-smudged a mark on Donna's left cheek. 'Still, I imagine they'll both be back for lunchtime. Sunday roast and all the trimmings? Ha! They wish. Tell you what, it's a trip to the Jolly Lock Keeper and the all-you-can-eat for a tenner today, my girl. Those days of my slaving over beef and Yorkshire pudding went with your dad, let me tell you.' Sylvia eased Donna's red hair behind her ears and flicked her fringe. 'And there was a note left for you last night, found it when your granddad woke me up, staggering in after you'd dropped him off. I didn't read it, but it's from those Carnes boys the Doctor was on about.'

Donna wanted to ask how she knew who it was from if she hadn't read it, but that way led to whole kettles of fish about notes from headmasters when Donna was twelve to letters from Martyn Hart when she was fifteen and who had opened which of those when they were addressed to the other, so she kept quiet.

Donna also had a pang for roast beef and Yorkshire pud, conjured up by her mum, covered in fantastic gravy. Dad carving. Granddad and Nanna over for the day, blathering on about train times and the car collectors club and long walks in Windsor Great Park. Suddenly she wanted to be ten again.

And wanted to cry.

'Mum?'

'What?'

'I miss Dad.'

And Sylvia Noble hugged her daughter in a way she hadn't for quite a long time. Then pulled away, almost as if she'd remembered that Sylvia Noble's preset was to be grouchy and uncompromising and not tactile and warm. Especially with her wayward daughter.

But it was enough of a moment to make Donna happy. Because it had been a real instinctive gesture.

'Can you call your granddad, please, find out when he's back and whether your Doctor is joining us at the pub.'

'And Netty?'

(Ooh, very bad thing)

'If we must.'

Eager to change the mood, Donna opened the front door to check on the weather.

'Mum, why d'you say Granddad's gone to the allotment?'

'What else does he do? It's either the veggies or Netty. When they're not one and the same.'

Donna shot her a look and Sylvia had the decency to apologise. 'Sorry. Get used to being on my own so much, I forget that I shouldn't say to other people things I say out loud to myself.'

'We'll worry about you and Netty later. Granddad's taken the car. Which he doesn't need for the allotment.'

Sylvia frowned. 'He didn't say he was taking it. Said he was going to meet the Doctor.'

'So you assumed it was at the allotment?'

'Like the other night, yeah.'

Donna was dialling her grandfather on his mobile, but it was switched off. The silly beggar was on his way to Copernicus, wasn't he? And he'd left Donna behind.

At which point that 'shot heard around the world' moment occurred.

Donna would always remember that she was in her dressing gown, standing at a slightly open door, a note from the Carnes boys in her hand (unread, by her at least), staring at a space where a car should have been, her mum just behind her. There was a fresh mug of tea by the Yellow Pages. Over the road, old Mister Lyttle was walking his dog. A small black thing of indeterminate breed that always smelled of wet fur. To the left, a real peripheral vision type thing, a blue van was parked.

And dominating the blue sky was a massive, ferociously awful pillar of pure bright light, the very edges suffused with a faint purple glimmer.

Donna heard her mum say, 'Oh my God, not again, not the sky on fire again.'

But it wasn't entirely on fire. Just this one column, accompanied by a sound like a gas flame on the cooker, but ramped up by ten thousand decibels.

Donna just knew that something awful was happening where that column of light hit the ground, somewhere to the west of Chiswick. Although she didn't know it then, all around the world, no matter what time zone, similar columns of heat energy were doing the same.

And in the sky, that leering face of stars was still up there, the hideous grin seemingly wider and broader than ever before.

'Mum, inside, now. Lock the doors, let no one in except me. Or Granddad. Or the Doctor. Especially the Doctor.'

'And why is he so special?'

'Oh, just say you'll do it, will you.'

'All right,' Sylvia muttered. Then: 'And where are you going?'

'I need to try and find him. Both of them actually.'

'Aren't they together?'

'That's what I'm worried about.'

'Well, you can't go out like that.'

Donna realised she still wasn't dressed and ran upstairs, throwing off her dressing gown when she was barely through the door of her room.

'Don't leave that lying on the floor,' Sylvia called. Donna picked it up, hung it on the door hook and sighed. 'Priorities, Mum,' she muttered.

Dressed in a T-shirt and an old tracksuit she couldn't believe she ever wore but knew would be warm, Donna headed back downstairs, grabbing a heavy coat.

Out in the street, she could hear people and cars revving up. Everyone had seen the pillar of light and now they were seeing that awful face in the sky.

Give it half an hour and it'd be panic on the streets, rioting, looting and police everywhere. She had to get out of London fast.

'No car,' she cursed to herself.

She opened the front door – that blue van.

So wrong. So wrong, Donna Noble. So wrong.

Then she was at the driver's window, looking at the seat. The dashboard. The lack of keys. The locked door.

Poor Miss Oladini had made it look so easy when she'd hotwired that car, but Donna didn't have a clue where to begin.

Great.

She tried the door just in case.

It was open.

She glanced up the street but no one in the mêlée of people was yelling at her or claiming the van as theirs. She hauled herself into the driver's seat and put her hand under the seat to adjust it. God knew why – she wasn't going anywhere, because no one in this day and age was stupid enough to put their keys under the seat of an unlocked van.

She brought up her hands, a bunch of car keys in them.

'And I want a tricycle and a pony and a lifetime's supply of milk chocolate,' she said aloud, putting her hand back under the seat just in case her Christmas wishes from when she was eight came true too.

No ponies, no bikes, not even a melted chocolate bar. But the keys – that was good.

She ramped the van into reverse, and seconds later she was on her way back down towards Chiswick High Road, planning her second journey out towards Essex in twelve hours.

She threw a last look in the wing mirror at her house as she swung the van around and then shot off, hoping that her mum hadn't seen her do this. Cos then there'd be hell to pay. And quite right too!

Before she had even got to the main road, the crowds were in the street, staring and pointing, and she could hear sirens from ambulances, police and fire engines all around her, all heading down towards the west, towards the M4. Towards where the pillar of light had struck the ground. She was heading towards London and that side of the street was relatively empty, even for a Sunday.

Donna's attention was drawn by the number of people outside the various electrical shops that dotted both sides of the street. Chiswick High Road had mostly been cafés and show shops when she was growing up, but this invasion of gadget shops was weird. She remembered the Doctor saying he'd met the Carnes boys in one.

All this went through her mind in a brief second, probably because there on the streets in front of her were Lukas and Joe Carnes.

Like they'd been waiting for her.

Literally.

Standing in the street. One minute, the road had been empty. The next, two lads were right in front of her.

Donna hit the brakes, and just avoided skidding to a halt, actually making quite a graceful stop, although a man behind her hit his horn.

'Yeah? What else didja get for Christmas, sunshine?' she screamed back at him. 'Shove it up yer—'

The passenger door opened, and Joe and Lukas clambered in.

'Joe says we need to be somewhere called Copernicus,' Lukas said quietly. 'He also knew you'd be here. At this time.'

'Course he did,' Donna replied, driving forward as the irate driver overtook her, one hand off the wheel and gesturing at her. Shrugging, Donna continued driving towards Hammersmith. 'Morning, Joe,' she called to the boy, who was now in the back.

Joe didn't reply but got something out of his pocket.

'What's that then? New MP3 thingy?'

'It's an M-TEK,' Lukas replied on Joe's behalf.

'You what?' Donna tried to sound interested, but wasn't. She was more focused on how they'd known she would be there.

'It told him where you'd be,' Lukas continued. 'It talks to him.'

That sort of answered her question, Donna decided, but annoyingly threw up a couple of dozen other ones. 'Is that how he knew the Doctor's name the other day, then?'

Lukas shrugged. 'Dunno. Man in the shop gave it to him. Said it was a demo version. Gave out about ten of 'em. Said Joe was the right person to have one. He didn't tell me till we'd got home and I found him downloading music onto it.'

That made sense to Donna, although it didn't really make any sense at all. When you travelled with the Doctor, you began to accept that things that didn't make sense really *did* make sense in a not-making-sense-to-normal-people kind of way.

So this M-TEK thing made Joe Carnes know things. Or it told him things. Things to attract the Doctor's attention.

'Didn't your dad ever tell you boys about accepting gifts from strange men?'

'My dad did,' Lukas said, glancing at Joe. 'Joe's dad didn't stick around long enough.'

Well, thought Donna, that's a conversation killer. She made a sudden turn into the Hammersmith roundabout that caused someone to toot their horn. Maybe it was the same driver as before, but she didn't know or care. She turned onto the Talgarth Road.

It was empty. Really empty. This was a big six-lane roadway towards Central London, via Earls Court then Knightsbridge, then Hyde Park and eventually into Piccadilly. It should've taken twenty minutes, maybe thirty to get to Piccadilly on a Sunday lunchtime, and that was without any road works. Donna did it in ten and she wasn't exactly speeding.

It was as if all the people in London were going away... no, going towards something. That light. They were all heading towards that.

Rubberneckers, eager to take photos on their mobiles and say 'oh look, we saw the carnage!' or something more sinister? In which case why wasn't she affected?

'Scuse me, boys, more law-breaking…' Donna got out her mobile as she drove and called her mum. No reply. That wasn't good news.

So here she was, in a stolen transit van, driving through a deserted London, off to darkest Essex to rescue her granddad and her friend from killers, unable to contact home, complete with the Children of the Damned at her side.

'Cheers, Doctor,' she said to no one in particular.

Some twenty miles away from Donna and the boys, there was a massive police and ambulance presence around the Ruislip Woods area, with even more emergency services arriving from nearby RAF Hillingdon.

The massive bolt of white energy had struck the woodlands – one of Britain's first protected woods – although there wasn't too much to protect right now. It had created a massive bowl-shaped crater about a quarter of a mile wide, decimating the trees, grasses and shrubbery. A small waft of smoke drifted on the morning air and crowds of startled onlookers huddled close by, partly out of amazement, partly out of shock, but mostly out of fear.

Was it a plane crash? An al-Qaeda bomb? Something from the RAF base gone wrong? Casualties? Oh my God, my kids were playing here? Has anyone seen my dog, a lab cross? Excuse me, have you seen my husband, he was out jogging? Have you seen

*that awful face in the sky? Is it a movie stunt? I never trusted that
IRA ceasefire…*

Police Sergeant Alison Pearce was trying to control
the crowds and her own officers and get the emergency
crews through. The Sunday morning shift had seemed
such a good idea. Three kids meant that doing night
shifts was out, but her mum could babysit on a Sunday
while she did her shift. Normally, she'd be home by
ten, see them asleep and get them off to school in the
morning. She'd already called home and warned her
beloved mother that grandparental care might be the
order of the next couple of days. The paperwork alone
on this would keep her busy. And that's assuming she
ever actually got away from the site.

'Oi, you, excuse me?' she yelled out to a young guy
who was trying to get under the red and white tape. 'Sir?
You can't come through…'

The man ignored her. Sergeant Pearce grabbed her
radio and called a couple of colleagues over as she
stepped under the line herself and hurried over to him.

'Welcome back,' he said to… well, to nothing. Just to
the fine white ash that had once been trees and goodness
knows what else.

'Sir, I must ask you to get back behind the line. This is
a crime scene.'

The man continued to ignore her, and Pearce noticed
that five other people had done the same thing all
around the perimeter. 'Guys,' she said into her radio,
'what's going on?'

One of her constables reported back. 'We couldn't
stop them, Sarge, they just got away from us.'

148

Pearce sighed and reached out to the man, but he was on his knees now, reaching out to the ashen ground. 'Welcome back,' he said again.

And his fingers connected with the ground as Sergeant Pearce reached out to his arm.

She felt a shock, small, electrical, but powerful, and found herself a good couple of feet away, flat on her back, shaking her head to clear it.

The man was standing now, back to the crater of ash. Pearce realised that the other people, now seven in total had done the same. It was like they were guarding the site.

The young constable who had spoken to her over the radio was at her side. 'You OK, Sarge?' he said, helping her up.

She pushed him away. 'I'm fine, Steve. What the hell is this?' PC Steve Douglas shrugged. Sergeant Pearce tried her radio but all she got was static crackle.

PC Douglas tried his. Same result. 'OK, this is dead weird,' he said.

Sergeant Pearce walked away and back under the line, telling Douglas to stay put and keep an eye on them. 'But don't go near them.'

She hurried over to a growing group of fire and police officers, which now included her superintendent. 'Sir, we have a problem,' she reported, and explained that seven people were guarding the crater.

Superintendent Shakiri frowned and started to move forward, towards the perimeter. 'Get the public further back, Sergeant. Move the line another six metres.'

She nodded, but still her radio wasn't working. Shakiri tried his. Nothing.

'It was working ten minutes ago,' he muttered.

'So was mine,' Pearce said. 'It must be something electrical.'

'Why'd you say that?'

She told him about being touched by the man and the shock she'd had.

'Get yourself seen to by one of the paramedics, Sergeant.'

'I'm fine, sir…' she started, but he waved her away. 'Delayed reaction, Sergeant. You'd tell anyone else to do the same. And if they say you're fine, I'll see you in five minutes.' He smiled at her. 'Please?'

Sergeant Pearce shrugged and walked towards one of the ambulances, while she listened to Shakiri yelling orders that the line was to be manually eased back.

As she reached the waiting paramedic, something… something instinctive made her look back. It was like a slow-motion moment in a movie, so much happened at once, she couldn't tell whether she saw it all or her brain pieced it together later.

A flash of purple light, like a bolt of electricity shot through the crowd of onlookers, flooring each and every one of them.

PC Steve Douglas vanished, although, for a split second, Pearce was convinced she saw him throw his arms up to protect himself from the purple flash, and she could see him – no, his *skeleton* – just for a second, then he was gone.

The seven 'guards', no longer hidden by the crowds, had stretched out their arms towards one another, and the purple electricity was connecting them all, like a rope.

Superintendent Shakiri threw himself down, dragging a couple of other officers with him in a rugby tackle, probably saving their lives.

There was a flash in the sky, like a sunburst, just for a second, and Pearce swore the whole sky flashed purple.

And then it was over. Sort of.

People were getting up and running further away. No one wanted to be near the electrical whatever-it-was. This was good in the sense that the public were going, but it was disorganised, and that was dangerous. If just one person fell... She remembered the story of a disaster in an East London tube tunnel during the war when it was being used as a shelter to hide from air raids. As the panicking public had scampered down the steps, one woman fell, bringing the whole crowd to the ground, killing almost two hundred people in the crush.

The panic going on right now, whilst not as confined, could be just as deadly. She saw Shakiri haul himself up, shouting to the officers around him to try and help the public. He threw a glance at where Steve Douglas had been standing – so he'd clearly witnessed it, too – and then back at her.

Waving the paramedic away, she ran over to join him at the scene. 'What the hell was that?' she breathed.

He pointed at the seven 'guards' around the crater. 'I imagine they wanted us all to go away.' He looked at the fleeing crowds. 'Any casualties?'

Pearce just looked at where her young PC had been. 'Would we know?' she said. 'There's nothing left of Steve Douglas.'

Shakiri caught her eye. 'And that's why we need to

know if there are others. If we hold them accountable for one death, we need to hold them accountable for any others.'

Both their radios crackled into life.

'Good morning everybody everywhere around the world.' It was a female voice, speaking clear, precise English. 'My name is Madam Delphi and I am the only voice you need ever listen to. I'm speaking to you all on every wavelength, every radio, TV, PC and PDA the world over. You have now seen what I can do and will continue to do. This planet is mine. You can all go back to your dreary little lives and wait for me to tell you what to do next. I now return you to your scheduled programming. Oh, sorry, except for those countries currently broadcasting any version of *Big Brother*. Sorry, all the contestants and presenters of that show, wherever they are, are dead. You can thank me later.'

The two police officers looked back at the seven people guarding the crater, that purple electricity still binding them together.

'Tell you one thing, sir,' Alison Pearce said, as she looked upwards to where it had all begun.

'What's that, Sergeant?'

'That scary face in the sky has gone.'

Miss Oladini was seriously thinking of handing in her notice. This was not a good enough job to be worth all this aggro.

Last night she'd been chased, had electricity chucked at her, been nearly blown up in a car and, worst of all, someone had nicked her bike. She hoped it was that redheaded woman who had been with her in the car, because that would mean she too had escaped the blast.

Miss Oladini wasn't entirely sure how she'd done it herself, but knew it had involved a lot of rolling along the ground, ignoring the heat and running into a bush and holding her breath for what seemed like an hour but could only have been a minute or two before her pursuers assumed both women were dead.

She had no idea what was going on at Copernicus, but her body had given in to the shock and she'd fallen unconscious in the grounds of the old mansion house, eventually waking up again, cold, damp and very hungry. And minus a bicycle.

She waited a while to see if anyone was watching her, then made her way back inside the house for warmth. After a couple of minutes, she found a couple of abandoned coats. She knew she was in shock. Her body needed protection and warming up.

She put on the coats, one on top of the other, then headed for a tiny closet. She could hide there, and its cramped conditions would help retain the heat she needed. She found a half-drunk bottle of water on a table top and took that with her, too.

After a couple of hours, she felt strong enough to venture out of her closet and see if the people were still there, see if Professor Melville was still with them.

She'd been creeping quietly down a corridor when she jumped, because a load of radios and TVs and a couple of desktops burst into life, and she listened to Madam Delphi's portent of doom, feeling cold again.

Now she had recovered enough from last night's ordeal, now it was daytime, it was time to get away from Copernicus. Forget Professor Melville and those people, this was too much for her to deal with, and she suspected that radio broadcast was connected. The police, maybe the army, they needed to know that something was going on here. She began to creep slowly towards the big staircase when a hand came out of nowhere and wrapped around her mouth, cutting off any noise she could make.

Miss Oladini thought this was it, she was going to die.

'Please be quiet, sweetheart,' said a voice in her ear. 'My name is Wilfred Mott, and I don't want to hurt you.'

He moved his hand away from her face, and Miss Oladini pulled away. She looked at the man, old, but not weak, clearly. His eyes burned with intelligence, but there was nothing threatening.

'Why are you here?' she asked bravely.

'My granddaughter was here last night. She told me about things going on here. I'm looking for the Doctor.'

'Granddaughter? Redhead?'

'That's Donna. You must be Miss Oladini? She thought you were dead, she'll be so pleased you're OK.'

Miss Oladini wasn't sure about this. Those people that had attacked her could know all this. But would they know about…?

'How did Donna get away?'

'On a bike. Was it yours? She left it near a police station somewhere. South Woodham Ferrers, that was it.' He smiled at her. 'She got home so late last night and I'd been waiting up. She told me everything that happened, and after I got her off to sleep I decided to check on this place myself.'

Miss Oladini frowned at him. 'You didn't believe her?'

'Course I did! Donna doesn't make things up. But I wanted to find the Doctor and keep Donna safe at the same time. She'd been through enough. So I left her sleeping and crept out of the house this morning.' He glanced at his watch. 'Right now she'll have worked that out and be creating merry hell, I reckon.'

Miss Oladini still wasn't convinced, but he didn't seem to have the zombie-ish approach of the rest of the people here. 'You're looking for a doctor? Which one? They're all doctors and professors here.'

'He came with Donna. Tall bloke, daft hair. Talks a lot of rubbish.'

'Sums up most of the Copernicus workers, frankly, Mr Mott.'

'Wilf. And no, he doesn't work here. He was asked to come here by a Professor Melville. That's why he and Donna turned up so late.'

'I spent most of last night hiding and being blown up, I didn't see Donna till we escaped. No idea if there was anyone with her at all. Sorry.'

Wilf seemed to deflate. 'Oh. I was so sure he'd be here. I think he's the only one who can save us from all that Madam Delphi stuff we just had to listen to.'

'Why'd you think that?'

'It's the sort of thing he does. Save us.'

'Some sort of vicar is he?'

Wilf laughed. 'No, no, not at all. So, where is everybody, then?'

Miss Oladini shrugged and explained she was thinking of getting away.

'Give me fifteen minutes,' Wilf said. 'If we don't find my friend, I'll drive you back home, how's that?'

Miss Oladini weighed up her options, and then agreed. There was, after all, no other way home as easy as this. And Wilf Mott didn't seem to be very threatening.

She led him down the stairs, through the shattered French windows and out into the back garden, pointing over at the radio telescope, explaining that was what the whole place was about.

Wilf nodded. 'That face in the sky, that was made up of stars, right? I reckon that observatory thing is where the Doctor would be.'

Miss Oladini shivered and pulled her coats tighter around her. 'I'm not sure,' she said quietly. 'I don't want to go back there.'

'Why not?'

But Miss Oladini couldn't explain. There was just something about it, something about the way the telescope had always seemed a safe place to work but now...

Wilf gripped her shoulder. 'All right, you wait here and I'll pop over and see if the Doctor's there. Won't be long.'

Miss Oladini watched as he wandered off. She shivered again. For one brief moment she had felt safe with this strange old man, and now she was alone again, she...

She caught up with him in seconds. 'Entrance, this way,' she said.

He smiled at her. 'Good for you, girl,' he said. 'Didn't fancy going in alone. To be honest.'

They smiled at each other.

'So, Donna's your granddaughter, then?' Miss Oladini said. 'Glad she got away.'

'Me too. Be lost without her. Family's an important thing to keep a hold of.'

Miss Oladini considered this. 'I don't know where my family are,' she said. 'Probably back in Nigeria.'

'How come you lost touch?'

She smiled. 'Oh, you know how it is, came to the UK for university, lost my status, stayed hidden here, signed on to the agency to find me work under a false name, usual stuff.'

'That's very brave of you,' Wilf said. 'Risky, too, working here.'

'Right under the government's nose,' she replied. 'Easiest way to disappear off the radar is to hide in plain sight. That's what my dad said last time I spoke to him.'

Wilf agreed. 'Used to say that about spies, during the war,' he said. 'Best way to infiltrate was to be seen, so no one got suspicious. Just become a member of society.'

'That's what I did. Look where it's got me. Frightened for my life.'

Wilf winked at her. 'You'll be all right.'

They were at the door of the radio telescope. It was slightly ajar and they crept in.

Professor Melville was dead. There was no doubting that, his neck was at such a strange angle, and although Miss Oladini had never seen anyone dead before, she just knew it. Her hand was over her mouth, stifling the cry in her throat. Wilf checked the poor man for a pulse, but gently lifted his hand away.

It looked like he had been working at the guidance systems for the array when he'd died. When he'd been *killed*, Miss Oladini thought. After all, people didn't break their own necks.

Wilf was climbing up the small ladder that led to the upper deck, where the telescope itself was housed. It wasn't an old-fashioned tubular telescope, but a series of computers arrayed across the room, linked to the radio dish on top of the building.

That had always disappointed Miss Oladini when she first came to work for the poor Professor. Somehow a giant telescope seemed more romantic than a computer bank.

She glanced back at his body, eyes staring open at the ceiling, and thought about his old mother. And his cat. And how scared she'd been of him the last time she had seen him. And now all she could think about was his cat.

And she began to cry for the first time since everything had gone wrong.

Donna punched at the radio buttons until she got a station. She didn't want music, she wanted news. It wasn't hard to find. All over the globe, massive beams of light had struck down, and been surrounded by people. Some observers were saying they were terrorists guarding a bomb site, some thought they were religious fanatics guarding something holy and special. Others reckoned it was aliens, coming to get those who had claimed to have been abducted and then returned with microchips in their heads over the last fifty years. The strange message from 'Madam Delphi', which everyone assumed was just an internet hacker trying to be funny, had started that one off…

'Irony is,' she said to the radio, 'that's the one that might be right!'

There didn't seem to be too many casualties but no one could get near the people actually guarding the craters. Britain, America, Russia, the Middle East, Asia, New Zealand, Africa, Greenland, nowhere was untouched. There seemed to be no connection between the people gathering to guard those craters: different ages, sexes, politics, backgrounds.

'Wonder if the Poles got attacked,' she mumbled after listening to the reports for a bit longer as they drove past the Tower of London.

'There was a mention of one in Germany,' Lukas said.

Donna smiled. 'I didn't mean Poles in Poland, I meant the North or South Poles.'

'Does it matter?'

'Yeah, it probably does. They seem to be heavily populated areas, rather than desolate. So there's something significant about that.'

'What?'

'No idea. But I'm thinking.' She looked at a sign saying A13 Tilbury. 'Essex thataway.' Then she shrugged. 'Not that I know exactly where I'm going. It was dark last night and I was thinking about the Doctor too much to note landmarks.'

'You want to take the A127,' Joe piped up. 'Three

miles along that after the M25 junction, then left into Meadow Lane, half a mile further on and right into Gorsten Road. Stay on that for six and a half miles, then left towards South Woodham Ferrers.'

'Oh yes, I remember that name,' Donna said. 'How do you know?'

'After passing under the railway bridge, you need to go eight miles on Tributary Road and as you get to the B8932, turn right into Allcomb Lane. Copernicus is two miles along there.'

Donna looked at Lukas, who just shrugged. 'He knew where to find you,' he told her. 'And what van you'd be driving.'

'That's creepy,' Donna said quietly, glancing at Joe in the rear-view mirror.

'That's Joe,' Lukas said. 'Thank God we're only half-brothers.'

'Don't say that,' Donna chided him. 'He's still your brother.'

'Yeah,' Lukas agreed. 'But if we were full brothers, maybe we'd both be weird. This way, I can translate if he starts speaking Italian.'

'Why would he do that?'

'Cos that's where his dad was from, according to Mum.'

And something flashed through Donna's mind. Something the Doctor had said at the dinner the night before, when she was helping Netty out and old man Crossland had thought he was barking. When he was talking about that Mandragora thing.

I first encountered it in the fifteenth century in Italy.

Something in Donna's head sparked. Mad dolphins! Course! It couldn't be that simple, surely… but then, he said it was five hundred years ago. Plenty of time for people from Italy to travel the world, have generations of kids… That man, last night at the telescope who zapped the Doctor, his accent could have been Italian. And he had gone on about genealogy…

'Any idea where in Italy?'

'Nah,' said Lukas.

'San Martino,' Joe piped up.

'Thought you might know that,' Donna said.

'Why?' asked Lukas.

'Cos I don't think him being all Super SatNav in the back there is a coincidence. I think something is using him to get us to that telescope thing for a reason.'

'You mean my little brother is an alien?'

'Don't sound too excited by that idea.'

'Nah, it's dead cool.' Lukas leaned closer. 'I always told Mum he was weird.'

'He's not an alien. But there might be something in his background that'll help the Doctor sort this out.'

Lukas glanced back at his brother, who was now listening to his M-TEK again. 'I don't want anything to happen to him though.'

Donna smiled at him. 'It won't, the Doctor'll make sure he's safe.' But inside, she wasn't quite so sure she could guarantee that.

The Doctor's eyes opened and Wilfred Mott swam into view.

He grinned. 'Hullo, Wilf.'

'Hello, Doctor,' said the old man, hauling him up. 'What you doing on the floor?'

'I was dumped. Deposited. Abandoned. How rude!' the Doctor mumbled. Then he grabbed Wilf by both arms. 'Where's Donna?'

'She's fine. Safe at home with Sylvia, thinking we're both up at the allotment.'

'Good. Excellent. Brilliant even. Now then, why did they leave me here?'

'That weird lot with the purple electricity?'

'Yes, that's them. Blimey, Donna doesn't miss much out, does she?'

'I made her tell me everything. Doctor?'

'Yes?'

'There's a dead man out in that officey area.'

The Doctor opened his mouth to speak, then stopped. 'I was afraid of that.' He followed Wilf out of the control room, casting one last look around, and squinting at some numbers on a screen. A moment later, he was laying Melville's dead body out on the floor, checking him.

'You must be Miss Oladini?' he said.

Miss Oladini nodded. 'How...?'

'I knew they were searching for you. Professor Melville asked me to try and find you. Keep you safe. And something about a cat?'

'Professor Melville was alive then?'

'Oh yes. They were forcing him to move the radio telescope into alignment with the Chaos Body up there.'

Wilf filled him in on the developments around the world.

'Madam Delphi?'

'She writes astrology columns in the papers,' Miss Oladini threw in.

The Doctor gave her a look.

'Sorry,' she said. 'Pointless information, I know.'

'Oh no it wasn't, Miss Oladini. Brilliant info, actually. Explains so much. If you are an alien super-being whose helix power is governed by the stars, then who better than an astrologer whose words are read and devoured by millions to use as your medium. We need to find this Madam Delphi and ask her where she gets her information from.'

'Why'd they kill Professor Melville?' Miss Oladini asked quietly.

'Mandragora is a great one for tools. All those people you saw last night? Tools. Tools to be discarded once they're of no use. I imagine poor Professor Melville did what he needed to do for them and they merely tidied up after themselves.' He put a hand of Miss Oladini's shoulder. 'A stupid, pointless waste of a good man and a friend. I'm sorry.'

She smiled at him. 'Is there anything I can do to help stop them?'

The Doctor looked back into the control room. 'Wilf, any sign of anyone else here?'

'No one.'

'I think they all left about nine o'clock this morning,' Miss Oladini added. 'I couldn't see much, but I heard them speak.'

'Car, Wilf?'

'Out the front.'

'Good, give it to Miss Oladini.'

'Why?'

'Yes, why?'

'Because you are alive, Miss Oladini, and I made a promise to a man to keep it that way. Go home. Wilf, phone?'

'It's dead, I never recharge it.'

'*Phone?*'

Wilf dug it out of his jacket pocket, and the Doctor sonicked it, then dashed back into the control room. A moment later, he returned and gave the phone to Miss Oladini. 'Recharged, should last a couple of weeks. Wilf, sorry, had to wipe the sim card.'

'The what card?'

'If you don't know, never mind. Miss Oladini, stored on that sim card are the coordinates the telescope is currently positioned to. I've also done a bit of nifty-swifty kinda stuff, meaning that when I call you on this phone, you are not to answer.'

'How will I know it's you?'

'Cos no one else is likely to ring it as they know its daft owner always keeps it off and lets the battery go flat.'

Wilf harrumphed.

'So,' the Doctor went on, 'when I call you, don't actually answer, but instead, press the hash key. And whatever happens, don't accidentally press it before I call you.'

Wilf wanted to know why, but the Doctor shook his head. 'Safer all round if you don't ask. Miss Oladini, do all that, and you may be responsible for saving the world. Possibly the entire universe. Wilf, keys.'

Wilf reluctantly handed them over and Miss Oladini gently put the phone into one of the pockets of her many coats.

'Good luck, Miss Oladini. And thank you,' said the Doctor. 'Off you go.'

She gave a last sad look at Melville. 'He was lovely,' she said simply.

'I know,' the Doctor said. 'Met him in 1958. He had a skiffle band, called The Geeks – I played washboard for him. Joe Meek was gonna produce the album. We called him "Ahab" cos his surname was Melville. To this day, I don't know what his real first name was.'

'Brian,' Miss Oladini said. 'That's what his personnel file said.' She smiled a sad smile at the Doctor as she headed off.

'Brian,' said the Doctor to the body. 'Goodbye, Brian.'

Wilf looked after Miss Oladini. 'Will she be OK? If those people are still watching us?'

'Nah, they've gone. She'll be fine, only lives locally, you'll be able to pick the car up next week. If we're all still alive.'

'Charming.'

'Always a risk.' He glanced up at the clock. 'I reckon we have about an hour to find out why they left me alive.'

'Then what happens?'

'The cavalry.'

Dara Morgan was standing in the penthouse of the Oracle Hotel, staring down at the elevated motorway below.

'They look like ants.' Caitlin was at his shoulder. 'Which is pretty much what they are.'

Dara Morgan opened his mouth, as if to speak, then shut it.

'You OK?' Caitlin asked.

He shrugged. 'I… I seem to remember something. Toy cars. I can see loads of little metal cars being played with by a child. The boy seems…'

'Familiar?'

'I was going to say "happy", actually.' Dara Morgan moved away from the window. 'Madam Delphi,' he said to the computer screens assembled across the desks lined up along one long wall. 'How are we doing?'

'It's fantastic,' the computer replied, waveforms positively glowing. 'All over the world, the children of Mandragora are linking up, protecting the sites of arrival. And MorganTech now controls eighty-seven per cent of the world's computer franchises.' Madam Delphi giggled. 'Stick that in your pipe and smoke it, William Henry Gates III.'

Caitlin started reading off some internet reports. 'There's a new cult of Mandragora in South America now,' she laughed. 'How far did Mandragora go back then?'

Madam Delphi's screens flashed. 'We went a long way. Ooh look, a whole lineage trace in Norway. Is there nowhere we haven't reached?'

Caitlin tapped a few more keys. 'And another in Zaire!'

'This truly is the dawning of the Age of Aquarius!' Madam Delphi cheered.

Dara Morgan was watching the cars again. And on the window, he was subconsciously drawing letters with his finger.

Caitlin glanced up. And frowned. Dara Morgan was drawing a C. And an F.

She was up and beside him instantly. 'Hey you,' she said, drawing him back. 'Madam Delphi has something to show us. A tenth of the world's population are joining us today. And when the M-TEK goes on sale this week, we'll have six times that many! Already the free prototypes we gave away have activated our sleeping brethren.'

Dara Morgan gave a last glance back towards the window, towards the M4 motorway and then down at the potential M-TEK sales. 'Once Murakami has sorted things out in Tokyo...'

'This world and all its people will belong to Mandragora!' said Madam Delphi. 'Oh, and I've just uploaded a whole new batch of horoscopes. How marvellous!'

Wilf had rescued an old coat from a room and brought it over to the observatory to cover Melville's dead body.

'Why'd they kill the poor man, Doctor?'

The Doctor was in the small control room, carefully studying the readouts, equally careful not to touch anything. 'He probably set all this up for the Mandragora Helix, then they didn't need him any more. It takes a percentage of its power to control people – better to save it for those it needs long term.'

'Such as?'

The Doctor turned away from the controls and ushered Wilf back towards the dead body, sonicking the door behind him. 'No one gets in or out until I say so,' he muttered. Then he smiled at Wilf. 'I wish I had an answer for you, Wilf, but truth is I've not got a clue. There's always a link between the people it enslaves and the people they enslave in turn. Right now, I have no idea what that is, or how your Madam Delphi fits in but I'm guessing she is linked to Mandragora.' Suddenly the Doctor slapped his hand to his head. 'Oh of course! I see it now! Wilf, what's the time?'

'Twelve thirty-five.'

'And you arrived here when?'

'About nine, I wanted to get here because—'

The Doctor held up a hand to quieten him. Then he counted down. 'Five. Four. Three. Two. And… one!'

At which point the outer door to the observatory was wrenched open, flooding the room with daylight.

Standing there, framed in it, was Donna Noble.

'The cavalry, as promised.'

Wilf hugged Donna. 'How'd you know we were here?'

The Doctor was leaning against the wall, arms folded, all nonchalant, but so proud. 'Aww, cos she's your granddaughter, Wilf, and she's brilliant.'

Donna ignored the compliment. 'I know what that bloke meant last night. And he was Italian. It's the Italians!'

Wilf looked from one to the other. 'What?'

'He said something about a man who licks mad dolphins.'

The Doctor nodded. 'I know.'

'Oh.'

'But let's see if we agree, go on.'

'Or,' Donna grinned, 'if I'm righter than you?'

'Improbable, but always possible. Fire away.'

'What he said was "The man. He licks mad dolphins." But he didn't say "mad dolphins", he said "Madam Delphi".' Donna smiled. 'Yeah, you'd guessed that, hadn't you?'

The Doctor nodded.

'I'm still working on the bit about him licking her,' Donna went on.

The Doctor smiled at her. 'Helix. It's the Mandragora Helix, Donna. But I don't know why the Italian bit is important... Oh, oh, yes, of course!'

'Fifteenth-century Italy. San Martino, perhaps?'

'What are you two talking about?' asked Wilf.

The Doctor looked at him. 'Potted history, Wilf. 1492, I met up with this alien energy from the Dawn of Time. Mandragora Helix, always striving to dominate the lesser species.'

'Who you calling lesser?' asked Donna.

'Fifteenth-century humanity, Donna. Not like twenty-first century humanity, oh no. You're far more sophisticated.' He smiled in a way that suggested this wasn't exactly how he perceived things, but she let it go.

'So, anyway,' he continued, 'I accidentally brought a fragment of the Helix energy to a small Italian principality called San Martino. I defeated it, very cleverly, by earthing it. Or so I thought. But that's quite literally what I did, shoved it into the ground, where it survived, trying to repair itself. Got into the land, into the water and ultimately into the people. A tiny biological entity attaching itself to chromosomes, DNA, whatever. Transferred from generation to generation until the whole kit and kaboodle of Mandragora shifts itself halfway across the universe and links up. Last time, it wanted to halt human progress. This time, Mandragora's realised that there's no stopping you, you'll be out there, flooding humanity across the stars in no time, colonies, empires, wars and peacetimes, until the end of time. So Mandragora says, "I'll have a bit of that, thank you," and glues itself to you for eternity. Great plan, it can manipulate you all for millennia to come.'

'So all over the world,' said Donna, 'diluted through breeding and whatnot, there are these descendents from San Martino all over the world. Thousands of them now, probably unaware half of 'em that they even have Italian blood in them. And Mandragora is controlling them.' She turned back to the Doctor. 'That's how Joe Carnes knew you were who you are. His dad's from San Martino.'

'How'd you know that?'

'Joe told her.' Lukas Carnes poked his head through the door. 'He's finished in the toilet, Donna,' he added as the two boys walked in.

'Oh yeah,' Donna smiled weakly at the Doctor. 'Say hi to my team of helpers.'

The Doctor was overjoyed to see them. 'That's how you found us, wasn't it? I thought it was unlikely you'd memorised last night's taxi route.'

'Like a guide dog, Joe is,' Donna said.

The Doctor put a hand on Wilf's shoulder. 'We're done here. Let's go home. Via Greenwich.'

'Greenwich?' Wilf frowned. 'Oh no. No, Doctor, don't involve Netty. Please!'

'I really think she can help, Wilf. I'm sorry.'

'Who's that?' Lukas was pointing at the coat-covered body in the corner.

The Doctor took a deep breath. 'A good mate of mine, Lukas. He died.' And he threw a look at Wilf. 'But he's the last friend who dies at the hands of the Mandragora Helix, I promise you.'

Donna took this in, remembering her promise in the van to Lukas about Joe. She hoped the Doctor wouldn't let them down.

As he passed her, he winked and smiled.

What was she thinking? This was the Doctor.

Of course everything would be OK.

How could it not be?

The journey back to London was uneventful, to say the least. Wilf sat in the front seat next to Donna, wincing occasionally as she almost clipped wing mirrors on parked cars. The Doctor and the two boys sat in the back once they'd shifted blankets, a water bottle and a toolbox.

The Doctor had found a paperback book under a seat called *A Dark and Stormy Night*, all about rich kings, pirates, frightened maids, strong cattle herders and a young girl found in the snow. The Doctor sympathised with the story's hero, a young hospital intern who tried to piece the disparate elements together.

After a while, he'd given up and thrown it to the boys. Lukas had eagerly started reading it, at the same time keeping a protective eye on Joe as the Doctor asked him about his long-lost dad.

He got no useful answers. Joe couldn't really remember going to the electrical shop on Friday afternoon – if it hadn't been for the free M-TEK prototype, he'd never even have known he'd been there.

'He has days like that,' Lukas muttered.

'What's an M-TEK when it's at home, then?'

Lukas turned back to the book while Joe showed the Doctor the small portable device. 'It's like an MP3 player that plays movies as well,' said Joe. 'It connects to the net, it's a phone and it's got a 160-gig memory, so you can keep stuff on it. It runs Windows and OSX 6 really fast.'

The Doctor nodded, impressed. 'Great things come in small packages,' he said, and promptly got out his sonic screwdriver and zapped the M-TEK with it.

Recognising that noise, Donna yelled back, 'Hope you're buying him a replacement.'

But the Doctor was frowning. The sonic had done absolutely nothing. Not even scrambled the stored music. 'That's…'

'Weird?' Donna offered.

'More than weird,' he agreed. He scrambled to the back of the van, found the toolbox, took out a hefty hammer and brought it down on the M-TEK. The crash of the hammer, the yell of outrage from Joe and Lukas's very loud curse nearly caused Donna to mount the kerb as they turned into the Blackwall Tunnel.

'Well?' asked Wilf.

The Doctor held the M-TEK up. 'Not a scratch, not a dent, nothing. That's good tech. Alien tech, but good tech. It's also impossible.' He smiled at the somewhat shaken boys. 'Oh, I do like a bit of impossible.'

'Anyone noticed anything odd?' Donna asked.

'We're still alive after you driving for an hour?' Wilf suggested.

'No traffic,' Lukas suggested.

The Doctor looked up. 'That true?'

Donna nodded. 'Loads of parked cars. I've seen three other cars actually moving since we left Copper Knickers. One of them kept flashing me, I thought he was cross about something.'

'Probably was,' said Wilf. 'You cut him up.'

'But I think he was trying to flag us down,' Donna ignored her granddad. ''Cos this is just mad. Where is everyone?'

'It's Sunday?' the Doctor suggested.

'It's South East London,' countered Donna, 'and we're not in the tenth century. There should be hundreds of cars.'

'I quite like it,' Wilf said. 'Everything peaceful. Take the next junction, sweetheart, Netty lives just off the main road.'

They pulled up outside Netty's house in silence.

Wilf got out and rang the doorbell, but there was nothing. He called for her through the letterbox and, after a second or two, the door opened and he was yanked in, out of sight.

Donna, in the front of the van, glanced at the Doctor. 'Didja see that?'

'It was Netty,' the Doctor said.

'How'd you know?'

'Aliens would never wear hats like that.'

The door reopened and Wilf emerged, followed by Netty in a green felt hat with a peacock feather in it, all very 1950s.

'You seen the news, Doctor?' asked Netty, hauling herself in and sitting herself next to Wilf.

He said he hadn't.

'Then the best thing we can do is drive through Central London.'

Intrigued, Donna restarted the van and off they went.

Through Greenwich, past the rebuilt Cutty Sark and all the markets and shops. Through New Cross, down the Old Kent Road, around the Elephant and Castle and over Blackfriars Bridge.

'Not a single soul,' Wilf said. 'No one.'

'The BBC were telling everyone to stay indoors. Fairchild has declared a state of emergency.'

'Fairchild?' asked the Doctor.

'Prime Minister,' Lukas said with a sigh. 'Don't you know anything?'

'I know lots of prime ministers,' the Doctor said. 'But in this century they come and go annually, I think. This one clearly makes no impression on history.'

Donna brought the van to a sudden halt and, very quietly, said, 'Oh.'

Those in the rear of the van leaned forward. 'Oh indeed,' the Doctor said.

Because they could go no further. They were on the Embankment, just down from Charing Cross station.

As were possibly a million other people. Standing. Still. Arms reaching up to the skies.

And all chanting quietly. 'Helix. Helix. Helix.'

'That's not good,' Donna said.

The Doctor passed her Joe's M-TEK. 'Call your mum, please.'

'Why?'

'Let her know we're safe and we'll see her tomorrow.'

'Priorities?' asked Donna.

'Keeping on the good side of your mum is a priority, Donna. For both of us. She'll be worried.' He turned to the Carnes boys. 'Then we'll phone your mother, she must be worried sick.'

'Won't be,' said Joe quietly. 'She'll be one of this lot.'

Wilf was about to ask why, but the Doctor shook his head. 'Now, Joe, just cos she's your mum, she's not in any danger. None of these people are, by the look of it.'

'She gave birth to him. Maybe she's got this Helix gene thing?' said Lukas. 'Thank God I'm the older one.'

Joe stared out of the van. 'What do we do to rescue her, Doctor?'

The Doctor smiled. 'That's the spirit, boys, remember we *can* save her. We can save all these people.'

Donna passed the M-TEK back. 'She says Chiswick's empty. I told her to stay indoors, drink tea and keep the TV on. I said to do whatever the BBC says unless it involves leaving the house or stopping drinking tea. She didn't see the funny side.'

'I'm not surprised,' said Wilf. 'Well, Doctor, what do we do?'

The Doctor was looking at the M-TEK. 'They gave

this to you, Joe, yeah? Have they given loads of free ones out?'

Joe nodded. 'On the forum, they said they were giving out a million free ones before tomorrow's launch.'

'I bet the target audience was of very specific genealogy, too. So, this thing goes nationwide tomorrow?'

'Worldwide,' Netty put in. 'I'm going to get one. I like things like that. Was going to wait a month or so, see if the home shopping channel did 'em cheap.'

'Oh I like that,' Donna said. 'Well, used to. When I had time. That Anis Ahmed did things for me…'

Netty laughed. 'So sexy…'

Wilf coughed. 'Anyway, getting back to the matter in hand. Doctor, we can't just park here.'

The Doctor was still playing with the M-TEK. 'Nothing is that well protected… If I can just rewrite some of the software…' The sonic flashed a couple of different shades of blue, the M-TEK gave a ping, and the Doctor cheered. Then stopped. 'I appear to have accessed a horoscope website. Ah, our old friend Madam Delphi.'

'She works for the people who made the M-TEK,' Lukas said. 'She writes her horoscope things for some of their papers.'

The Doctor stared at the youth. 'You what?'

'MorganTech, they make everything these days. Run TV stations, newspapers, the works.' Lukas shrugged. 'Think a cross between Bill Gates, Rupert Murdoch and Richard Branson and you have Dara Morgan.'

'And who's he when he's at home?' asked the Doctor.

'He runs MorganTech. Been around for a few years

now. We did some research on him at school, but there's not that much out there. He's not keen on unauthorised biogs.'

The Doctor looked at the group in the van. 'So let me get this right. We have beams of light hitting the ground, hypnotised people chanting to the stars thanks to a newspaper astrologer telling you she's changing the world, new gadgets given away free to people who are of Italian descent and no one thinks to tell me they're all connected?'

The others looked at each other. Donna spoke eventually. 'We can't be expected to make the leaps of logic you do, you know.'

'They're not leaps, they're clearly defined paths of evidence and… oh, never mind. Where do I find this MorganTech?'

'Near where we live,' Lukas said. 'In Brentford.'

'Oh that's right,' Wilf said. 'They have that big office and hotel complex on the Golden Mile.'

'And the guy in charge is called Dara Morgan?'

'Yup.'

'Course he is,' the Doctor muttered. 'He would be. Lukas, I want you to try and remember everything you can about him, all right?' The Doctor chucked the M-TEK onto the floor, and Joe went to scoop it up. 'Leave it alone, Joe – it's dangerous.'

He sonicked the back of the van, and the doors sprang open. 'Come on, we're not going to get past this lot, we need to walk and find new transport.'

'Doctor,' Wilf protested. 'Netty's…'

'Hey,' Netty said. 'I can walk as well as you can,

Wilfred Mott.' She linked her arm through his. 'We can support each other.'

He smiled down at her.

And Donna was going to do the same until she saw the look on the Doctor's face.

Like it had been at dinner the night before.

He was looking at Netty… strangely.

Donna pulled the boys closer to her. 'Stick with me,' she told them, 'and we'll help the Doctor put an end to all this.'

'Donna,' the Doctor said suddenly, and in a way Donna had got used to. It was his warning voice.

Between them and the chanting crowd was a group of people. People Donna recognised from the night before, at the Copernicus Array.

'Not good?'

'Not good.'

'How did you reprogram the M-TEK?' asked the little man at the front of the group. Donna remembered him, too. He had led them, and she realised from his accent he was, of course, Italian.

'Talent,' the Doctor said.

'That is not part of the plan,' the little man said. 'We cannot allow a weak link in the chain.'

'Oh, sorry,' the Doctor said, indicating with his hand for the rest of his group to move away, slightly behind him, leaving him stood between the Mandragora-powered group and the van. 'I left it in the back. Do you want me to get it?'

'You will leave it,' the Italian said, as he pushed past the Doctor and clambered into the van.

The Doctor smiled at the rest of the group. An elderly duo to one side, four younger people at the back, a heavily built man to the left.

'I wonder how many of you are actual San Martino descendents, and how many are just their... slaves? Helpers? Unwitting participants in the murder of innocent professors at observatories? If you can fight Mandragora, maybe we can—'

The Doctor hit the tarmac hard as the blue van exploded into flames and debris.

Donna and the boys were already running, Wilf and Netty, staggering after them.

Good.

He glanced at the funeral pyre for the little Italian man that had once been a van.

'That's one way of eliminating the weak M-TEK, I suppose,' he said. 'Bit OTT if you ask me, though.'

And he got up, to be surrounded by the group. The burly man seemed to be their new leader and when he spoke, the Doctor recognised a strong Greek accent. 'Madam Delphi wants to see you.'

'Well, all right, but I want to check my friends are OK.'

'They're coming too.'

'Aw, I'm not sure I agree to that part of the deal.'

'Or we kill you now,' the Greek added.

At which point Wilf, Netty, Donna and the boys emerged from hiding and were quickly rounded up.

The Doctor sighed. 'I think that was probably a bluff,' he said to Wilf. 'They wanted me alive, remember?'

'We're in this together,' Wilf said. 'When I was in the paras, we never left anyone behind.'

The Doctor nodded. 'Oh well, now we're all here. Got a firm's coach?'

'We walk,' said one of the older people, an American woman.

'It's a long way,' Donna said.

One of the younger men shrugged. 'It'll keep us all fit, then.'

And they began the walk across London.

Everywhere they went, little groups of people were together, chanting to the skies.

Others could be seen, hiding, scared, occasionally looting shops, probably assuming this wasn't going to be cleared up any time soon, and that food would become scarce.

'It's like the Blitz,' Netty said at one point, as they walked through Leicester Square.

'Without the bombs and collapsed buildings,' the Doctor said. 'Thank goodness.'

The Doctor allowed his group to separate slightly, Donna noted. She was bringing up the rear with the boys, and Wilf was getting tired, and was only a few steps ahead. Behind her, the Greek man and older Americans. Ahead of the Doctor, the four younger people.

The Doctor was with Netty, having swapped places with Wilf, his arm now linked with hers.

Donna couldn't hear what he was saying, but Donna could tell from the urgency he gave off in waves and the lack of response from the old lady other than the odd nod, that they weren't really discussing London's architecture.

She almost asked her granddad what he thought it was about, but didn't. Because if it went wrong, if it all turned out bad, she didn't want him blaming the Doctor for anything.

Donna realised this was the first time she'd actually found herself questioning the Doctor's actions for quite some time. And she didn't like it.

A couple of hours passed. They had been allowed to stop occasionally, the younger people sorting out food (usually by using their Mandragora powers to blow doors off shops and nick stuff).

At one point, the Doctor and Netty had sat together in a deserted burger place, while the boys munched on cold chips and muffins. Netty had found some paper on a clipboard and was writing something on it, and the Doctor was nodding.

Wilf asked Donna whether there was any point in trying the microwave ovens, and when she glanced back Netty was alone, and the Doctor was trying to talk to the Greek man.

There wasn't time for microwaving burgers, as they were told to start walking again, despite the Doctor's protestations.

The boys were soon tired again. Netty and Wilf were very tired indeed. Donna was utterly exhausted, but the Doctor... he just kept going. He had Lukas and Joe up front with him now, trying to take their minds off it all by giving them a history of Cromwell Road and the various buildings as they marched along it.

The old American couple by rights ought to have been dead on their feet, but no, they were always there, one or other, sometimes both, with their arms pointing forward, ready to use their Mandragora power as she'd seen at the Copernicus Array the night before.

It was dark by the time they reached Hammersmith, and Donna reckoned it would take another hour or so to reach Brentford. Possibly longer, as Netty and Wilf were stopping more and more often.

'My granddad is very old,' she said at one point to the Greek man, eliciting an outraged, if exhausted, 'Oi, I'm fine' from Wilf.

The Greek man just shrugged and said that Madam Delphi would not be kept waiting.

It wasn't a cold night, but neither was it the height of summer and, by the time they started walking down the carless, people-free Great West Road, it was nearly midnight.

Donna was with the Doctor. Wilf and Netty were with the Carnes boys.

Wilf tried to keep their flagging spirits up with tales of his exploits in the parachute regiment, like he'd done for Donna when she'd been their age, albeit on long car trips rather than painful hikes across scary cities.

'Why don't you let these people go home?' the Doctor suggested, stopping suddenly. 'Madam Delphi only wants me, I'm sure. Look, we're in Chiswick. Let Donna take Wilf and Netty home. And let the boys head off, too. Please?'

The Greek ignored him and kept going.

'Not that Gramps or I would leave you for a moment,' Donna hissed at him as she walked to catch the Doctor up, 'but why do you think they do want all of us?'

The Doctor looked her in the eye. 'Insurance,' he said simply. 'Threaten to hurt me, no use. Anyway, they need me alive for whatever reason. Threaten to kill you, it's leverage. Sorry.'

'Don't be,' Wilf said. 'We chose to get involved with all this. I'm proud to stand beside you, Doctor. So are my soldier boys here.'

The Carnes lads nodded, Lukas a little more enthusiastically than Joe, it had to be said.

The Doctor looked at Netty. She was starting to walk erratically, drifting towards the central reservation of bushes.

'It's the exhaustion,' the Doctor said sadly as Wilf headed over to guide her back to the group. 'Her mind's going again like last night.'

'Then why'd you bring her?' Donna said a little more aggressively than she'd intended.

'I didn't expect to be walking,' the Doctor said. 'I'm sorry.'

Donna let herself drop back a couple of steps. Something in the Doctor's plan had gone wrong, and he was actually worried.

That wasn't a good sign.

Suddenly a set of headlights flashed ahead of them and, as one, the Doctor's group shielded their eyes. A small minibus screeched to a halt in front of them.

'Hey,' Donna yelled. 'You gotta help us!'

The Doctor went to stop Donna, but it didn't matter. The minibus door opened and a woman called out.

'Hop in, folks,' she said in a cheery Irish accent. 'Madam Delphi's waiting.'

One by one, they piled in.

'You couldn't have come about three hours ago?' Wilf grumbled as he helped a confused Netty up the steps into the vehicle.

The woman laughed. 'I'm Caitlin and, on behalf of MorganTech, I apologise for your discomfort. But that's nothing to what's coming. And no, Madam Delphi believes exhausted prisoners are far more malleable than fit and able ones. The only reason I'm here is it's nearly midnight. And time's getting on. Hold tight!'

Caitlin did a U-turn and roared off down the A4, towards the Brentford business area known as the Golden Mile.

'Here we are,' Caitlin said, slowing down.

Ahead, Donna saw the Oracle Hotel loom out of the darkness, lights on in every window.

'Ha!' the Doctor laughed. 'We're going to see the Delphi at the Oracle. Very witty. Not.'

'It's midnight,' Caitlin announced as she pushed the minibus doors open. 'Today is now Monday. The universe will never be the same again.'

And she smiled.

And Donna shivered.

MONDAY

The Doctor, Donna, Wilf and their friends were led up to the penthouse suite by Caitlin, who kept her hand resting on the butt of a revolver tucked into the waistband of her trousers.

As the Irishwoman pushed the penthouse doors open, the Doctor marched in and glanced around. He began clapping slowly when he saw what was inside.

'Madam Delphi, I presume?' he said. 'Of course. You're not a real person, are you? You're a computer! Well, I say a computer, more of an artificial intelligence, housing an ancient malevolence that should never really have been freed from its dimension. How are you, Mandragora? It's been a few centuries.'

'This… form is oh-so much more capable than a fleshy human body, Doctor,' Madam Delphi said. 'As a Time Lord, as someone who can stand so much more spatial and temporal trauma, your body is just what, if you'll excuse the excruciatingly bad pun, the Doctor ordered.'

The Doctor said nothing.

'You've heard that one before, haven't you?' Madam Delphi asked.

The Doctor and Donna now stood at the front of their exhausted group, Wilf, Netty, Lukas and Joe hovering a few steps behind. Facing them, in a protective circle around the Madam Delphi computer, were Dara Morgan, Caitlin and the Mandragora converts who had walked them there.

'Oh, hullo,' said the Doctor, as if addressing a meeting of the WI. 'This all looks very impressive. Nice room. Nice hotel. Nice gesture.' He pointed to where the old American lady had raised her arm in the now-recognisable Mandragoran position to fire a bolt of lethal Helix energy. 'Although a bit unfriendly.'

'I do apologise. You just can't get the staff,' the computer's feminine voiced boomed out from speakers dotted around the room. 'Welcome to my hotel. Can I recommend the gym? Great pool, I understand.'

'What's the bar like?' Donna asked. 'I mean, not exactly five-star without a good bar, is it?'

'Ah, Donna Noble, welcome to you, as well. I think you'll find we offer four bars, three restaurants and an à la carte room service 24/7.' Madam Delphi then chuckled. 'Gotta say, though, we aspire to a greater recognition than just five stars.'

The Doctor nodded. 'Well, I reckon you're looking for about five million. What do you think, Donna?'

'Gotta have good service to get five million stars, Doctor. Do you remember that hotel on Cassius? That was a proper five-star hotel.'

'Oh yes!' the Doctor grinned at her. 'And they understood customer relations, too. Remember when we had that little problem with the lizard?'

'Do you get lizard problems in Brentford, Madam Delphi?' Donna asked. 'Cos if there's lizard problems to be solved, I don't think it's that great a hotel.'

'The Oracle is—' started Dara Morgan, but Madam Delphi shushed him.

'The Doctor and his sweet friend are just playing for time, Dara. Trying to figure out how to stop us, how to get out of the Oracle alive, how to "help" their precious planet Earth.' Madam Delphi took a beat then continued, more silkily and thus slightly more menacingly. 'But you really aren't going to stop us, Doctor. I offer no guarantees about people getting out alive. And, from my perspective, helping Earth is precisely what we are doing.'

The Doctor walked towards the group, and they parted, almost reverently, so he was now looking straight at the screens of the computer.

'Last time we had a chat, I sent you into the darkness, licking your wounds. Remember that?'

'Of course.' Madam Delphi's sine waves pulsated ferociously. 'I have waited so long for a chance to get to you personally. To make you pay.'

'Oh, not the old revenge on the poor Time Lord schtick, Mandragora? I mean, you're better than that. Go on, give us a better reason.'

Madam Delphi giggled. 'It's not the first time since 1492 that the Mandragora Helix has been to Earth, you know.'

'Yup, that I do know. The Sacred Mountain of Xi'an, if I remember? Then there were the Orphans of the Future, all that white and crimson cowl stuff. Oh, and the Mandrake nightclub stuff, now that was pretty good, I have to say. But each time, it's just been a fragment of Helix energy, hasn't it, a little sparkler sent out to test the waters. This time, we've got the whole bonfire. So why now? Why send me little psychic-paper messages to get me involved, to bring me here… ahhh… Yes, you wanted to get me here. This exact day, this exact time. Why?'

'The stars are aligned,' Dara Morgan said.

'I'm talking to Madam Delphi, thank you, not the hired help.'

'How dare you—' Dara Morgan began.

'Oh, do belt up,' the Doctor snapped. 'I mean, who are you anyway?'

'I am Dara Morgan. I set up MorganTech. I created the M-TEK, I devised—'

'Oh please, you did nothing that the Mandragora Helix didn't tell you to. No, who are you really? Who did the Helix take, distort, manipulate and totally screw up before reimagining you as Dara Morgan?'

'What?'

'Lukas?' the Doctor barked. 'My research assistant,' he explained quietly to Madam Delphi. 'Donna was busy. Family matters.'

Donna frowned. Not that he was getting Lukas Carnes to do his research, but why he'd said 'family matters'. She threw a look at Wilf but he shrugged. Then she glanced at Netty, staring intently at the stand-off before them. When Donna looked back at the Doctor, she recognised a look in his eyes. A look that, if given voice, would have been some variation on

'I'm sorry. I'm so, so sorry.'

'No,' she mouthed. 'Don't you dare!' but the Doctor's attention was back on Dara Morgan.

'All over the world, Dara Morgan, billions of people will fall victim to this alien consciousness you've given access to the world. And that's going to happen today.'

'I know,' smiled Dara Morgan. 'How brilliant is that?'

'Well, it's brilliant from the point of view of your M-TEK being a pretty damn brilliant piece of technology, augmented by alien know-how and distributed quite magnificently to people who, I imagine, had no idea what it would do to them today.'

'Not a clue.'

'There's a lot of blood on your hands, Dara Morgan. If I were a policeman, I'd have you arrested but, as Lukas will now explain, that's not possible.'

'Dara Morgan came to prominence eight years ago, making his first claims about MorganTech on a news special, broadcast live on 31 December 1999.'

'End of the millennium, neat.'

'Before that, there's no trace of any such person. MorganTech was registered as a private limited company at 5.29pm that same day.'

'So who were you before Mandragora got hold of you? Before reimagining itself as a human, becoming the anagrammatical Dara Morgan?'

'Oh, I get it now,' Wilf called out. 'That's very clever.'

'Yes, thank you, Granddad,' Donna hissed. 'But let the Doctor focus.'

Before anyone could stop him, the Doctor put his hands to either side of Dara Morgan's head, fingers pressed against his temples and whispered, 'Open the locked doors, and let yourself out.'

The assembled acolytes took a step towards the Doctor, and Madam Delphi pulsed menacingly. 'Stop him,' she said.

In his mind's eye, the Doctor could see an image. A dark night, cold, damp. He was walking down a lane, hedges high on either side, rain trickling down his neck.

He shivered. He was angry… No, not angry. Hurt. Bewildered. She'd said no. No to what? Who was she? In his hand was a box, soft, velvety. And inside it, yes, he could imagine it. Silver band, plain diamond. All he had been able to afford. And she'd said no. Said that she needed to get away from Derry, wanted to go to Sydney. Or San Diego. Or anywhere other than close to him. How had he got her so wrong? How hadn't he seen this coming? How was it possible to love someone that much, so that every time she walked into a room, every time she spoke, smiled, laughed, his heart would leap. That just knowing she was in the kitchen, in the bathroom, in the hallway was enough to send those fantastic, amazing, wonderful thoughts rushing through him? Yet when it came to it, when he'd said 'I love you', she'd said she wanted to get away. No 'I love you too, but…' No 'Thank you, but I'm sorry.' Just an 'Oh my God, are you for real? No, I'm getting away from Ireland as soon as possible. I don't want to be tied to anything here!'

It was as if someone had ripped everything out of him that mattered and walked all over it.

You're not the first person to fall in love and be rejected, he told himself rationally.

But he didn't want to be rational. What was rational about being in love anyway? What was rational about offering yourself up to someone only to be squashed?

And here he was, lost and alone. Everyone had said she wasn't interested. Everyone had tried to say he was wasting his time. But when you're in love, you grasp at anything, you believe that one day you'll wake up and they'll say, 'You know what, I'm wrong, you're right, you are the person for me.'

But that hadn't happened.

It never happened.

Instead he'd seen the lightning ripping across the night sky as he stumbled along the road, tears mixing with the rain, thinking that all he wanted to do was be home now.

Home.

Ten minutes' walk, max.

More lightning. Blue, white and purple…

Purple?

It struck the ground in front of him, knocking him backwards.

He remembered seeing the little box with the ring vanishing in a sudden conflagration, literally and metaphorically drawing a line under that part of his life.

He felt as if he were on fire, too. All he could see was purple light, surrounding him now, blotting out the hedges, blotting out the road, the darkness, the rain.

And then the voice. All around. In his head. Coming from the sky and his heart at the same time.

'It is your time. Callum Fitzhaugh is no longer relevant. Now you have a greater cause.'

The voice stayed with him long after the purple fire had gone, over days and weeks as he willingly gave himself a new purpose.

The next morning he touched the keypad on a cashpoint machine and it spurted out two hundred pounds. Eight more cashpoints that morning. Then more in different towns. Then he set up an account. He manipulated the online banking, untraceable movements because he fed figures into the computers that erased all traces of his actions.

Within three weeks, he was a multimillionaire. He had buildings all over the world. He owned companies which he then closed or merged and, within a month, MorganTech had come into existence due to the manipulating influence of the voice in his mind that told him how to do it.

Next he had put together the computer system that would change his destiny. Somehow the voice guided him as he built Madam Delphi, felt that voice in his head transfer into the hardware, somehow, creating artificial life on a scale unheard of before now.

'I need you,' the voice had soothed. 'Now and for ever. I need a human interface, a connection to the world of flesh and blood. An avatar in reality.'

So Dara Morgan had been created.

He remembered coming from a rich family of bankers and investment traders. His parents died in a private plane crash, and MorganTech had passed to him when he was just 21.

He remembered more false memories, events, people, qualifications and parties. None of them real, but each time he imagined a part of the fictional history, it came true. The voice showed him how a society that relied on computers for information, that no longer used paper and ink to keep records, could so easily be manipulated in accepting the history, the lies, the fabrications you told it via the keyboard were true.

He remembered the voice telling him how to develop the M-TEK over a few years, so that the market would trust in it. Trust in MorganTech. This was a long game.

And he remembered seeing her in a street in Dubai one afternoon.

She was with a couple of men, going through a sheaf of documents in a roadside café.

He had listened as the men had explained that they needed to think about whatever deal they were doing and moved away. Then he went to sit beside her.

She looked up, initially intrigued, then surprised and then shocked. Eventually she found her voice. 'Cal?'

'Not now,' he said. 'Dara Morgan.'

She laughed, a soft, gorgeous, beautiful laugh that brought back all that love he'd felt years earlier.

But the voice in his head hissed, 'No. Remember the ring. Remember the tears and the pain. Do not give in now, Dara Morgan.'

'You do look like him, Cal,' she said. 'What brings you to Dubai?'

'Mandragora will swallow the skies,' he said. 'Let me show you, Cait.'

He took her hand, and her eyes flashed with violet

Mandragora energy. Then she had opened the folders she had been going over with the businessmen earlier. 'Sign here please, Mr Morgan.' And he did, because the voice told him to.

Within an hour, MorganTech owned a chain of five-star hotels across the world, and Caitlin had become his first convert.

With a gasp, the Doctor pulled away from Dara Morgan, who immediately collapsed to the floor.

The whole thing had taken less than a second in real time but, to the Doctor, it had seemed like forever.

He staggered away from Dara Morgan as the rest of the Mandrogara-influenced group turned on him, arms raised, ready to deliver the death blast.

'No!' Madam Delphi's sine waves were bouncing up and down on her screens. 'No, I need that body. It's why I have waited these long centuries for the Doctor to present himself. The last of the Time Lords, possessed by Mandragora Helix energy, animated by me!'

The disciples lowered their arms.

And little Joe Carnes wrestled away from his brother and ran to the Doctor. 'No,' he yelled. 'Leave him alone.'

Lukas was at his side in a second, and then Donna and Wilf were there, too.

They stood between him and the Mandragora-possessed computer.

'Yes, thank you all,' the Doctor said. 'But not really necessary.' He smiled at Madam Delphi. 'So what a lot of choices. Kids no one would take seriously, an old man with a heart condition who could drop dead at a moment's notice, his friend Henrietta, an expert on the stars…'

He threw a look behind them all, a look only observed by Donna.

Henrietta Goodhart was still by the door, as if trying to make sense of what was going on.

The Doctor was looking at her with a mixture of sadness and… what was that, Donna wondered. Panic? Desperation? As if he were willing her to say or do something?

But it was no good. Netty wasn't with them at the moment.

'The lights are on, but no one's driving.' The sort of thing Donna could imagine her mother saying. A horrible phrase, but one Donna couldn't disagree with right now. And it was as if the Doctor thought Netty had let him down, somehow.

'Donna,' the Doctor hissed. 'Your mobile. Now.'

She pushed it into his hand and, keeping an eye on Madam Delphi, he expertly scrolled through her address book.

'Donna?'

'Yes?'

'Why isn't your granddad's number in here?'

'Cos he never turns the bloody thing on. What's the point?'

'Oh great. Thanks.'

'Why are you ringing him? He's standing here.'

'His phone is in Essex. I need to call it.'

Donna closed her eyes, imagining her fingers on the keypad and hissed the numbers at him. As she said each number, he pressed the key. When he heard the call go through, he hung up.

'I hope you're right, cos if you're not…'

'Someone just got a strange call?'

'And the world will end. But hey-ho, it's been fun.' He passed the phone back to her.

'You won't get him,' her grandfather was saying to the computer. 'This man is brilliant, he's saved this planet, the whole universe, probably, more times than we've had hot dinners. You'll have to go through us to get him!'

God bless Granddad, but Donna seriously doubted that was going to stop Madam Delphi. The Doctor needed something from Netty, Donna was sure of that. So he needed to be bought time.

'You want a body to inhabit that's been round the galaxy, lady,' she said, 'take mine. Oh, I might not have two hearts or hair that defies fashion, but this body's seen a bit of outer space action.' She pushed the Doctor right behind them now, so he was closer to Netty.

Madam Delphi's screens pulsed again. 'Noble by name, noble by nature, is it?'

'Oh, like I haven't heard that before. One night when Neal Bailey decided to get frisky at the Odeon, he muttered in my ear, "Now cracks a noble tart, how about a good night sweet Donna." I clumped him one where it hurts and walked out. Mind you, I reckoned he knew his Shakespeare and should've got Brownie points for originality. My dad didn't agree and bopped him on the nose down the pub the next week.' Donna smiled sweetly at the computer. 'Ever had a bloke come on to you? No, course you haven't, cos you're all electrics and wires and stuff. All alone, aintcha? That why you're doing all this, is it? Looking for love? Should've gone for the Lonely Hearts angle, instead of the astrology bit.'

Wilf tugged his granddaughter's arm. 'You'll make it cross.'

'Really, Granddad? That had never occurred to me.' She winked at him. 'I know what I'm doing.'

Madam Delphi pulsed angrily. 'Wish I could get my head around why the Doctor always surrounds himself with silly humans. I mean, what purpose do you serve? Other than sacrificial lambs. How many travelled in his TARDIS before you, Donna Noble? And what happened to them? I mean, you reckon you're going to travel with him for ever. You think you're the first to believe that? Course you're not. But you're here and they're not. Wonder what happened to all of them, then?'

Donna wasn't going to let this get under her skin – mainly cos that was a question she'd asked the Doctor before and she'd been more than satisfied with his response.

But it clearly struck a chord with her granddad. 'Sweetheart, that's a good question.'

'Really, it's not right now, is it?' she snapped back.

'Is there a churchyard with tombstones, all lined up with their names on them, d'you think, Donna?' said Madam Delphi. 'Got a plot of land saved for you, has he?'

'Maybe,' Donna replied. 'I don't much care, to be honest. I live for the here and now. And right here, right now, all I can be bothered to worry about is stopping you and your little army of zombies here.'

'Destroy them,' Madam Delphi said, so matter-of-factly, so casually, that it took Donna a second for it to sink in.

But sink in it did when the disciples, as one, raised their arms, ready to fire their bolts of energy.

Nothing happened.

'Destroy them!' shrieked the computer.

Still nothing happened.

'Destroy him,' Madam Delphi demanded, but the disciples did nothing except frown and look around themselves in surprise. It was as if they'd just awoken from a dream.

'Ah,' said the Doctor, 'that'll be me. Well, actually if I'm being honest, it'll be a lovely lady called Miss Oladini – never got her first name, very rude of me. Anyway, she's just knocked your alignment off a bit, cancelled out all the power you have over the descendents of San Martino, en masse. *Clos, kaput.*'

'*Finito,*' Donna said in a cod Italian accent.

'And that's not all!'

Donna looked to her left. Dara Morgan was standing to one side, a laptop in his hands, his fingers flying over the keys as he typed one-handed.

'I've sent out a cancellation signal via the net to the M-TEKs everywhere. As soon as they are synced with computers, instead of downloading your orders, they'll install a virus, which will defrag the platform, and erase their memories completely.' Dara Morgan tapped the return key one last time. 'And I've password protected it.'

'I'm a megalomaniac supercomputer, linked to

billions of electronic outlets throughout the world, you silly little man. You really think you've stopped me? I'm disappointed in you, Dara Morgan.'

Dara Morgan shrugged. 'Stopped you for good? Doubt it, but I've certainly slowed you down, so the signal won't be activated in ten minutes. Probably not for a few days now – plenty of time for the Doctor to stop you.' Dara Morgan smiled. 'And my name is Callum Fitzhaugh.'

A deep electronic sigh came from Madam Delphi. 'Caitlin?'

And the Irish girl, Callum's beloved who had rejected him nearly ten years before, drew her revolver from her waistband and raised it.

'Caitlin, don't,' Callum yelled. 'Fight the Mandragora influence. Remember who you really are!'

Caitlin frowned. 'Cal?'

'Yes, it's me!'

Caitlin shrugged. 'Never liked you then, don't much like you now.'

And she fired one bullet that went through Callum Fitzhaugh's brain and out the other side.

He was dead before he hit the carpeted floor.

The newly awoken disciples screamed and yelled in confusion and started to run out of the room.

'Go with them,' Donna hissed to the Carnes boys. 'Get out of here – Lukas, you get Joe home. Don't stop running till you get there.' She turned to Wilf. 'You too.'

'Blow that, Donna my girl. I'm too old to run and I'm here with you to the end. Told your father I'd look after you, and by God I will.'

It occurred to Donna that the Caitlin woman could have opened fire by now, so she looked to see what she was doing. She had placed the gun on the desktop and now sat facing Madam Delphi's screens.

The Doctor walked past Donna, almost incidentally easing Netty into Wilf's arms, muttering, 'Hold her tight, Wilf. Like your life depends on it.' He then crouched down beside Caitlin, snaking his hand out for the gun.

'Take it,' she said quietly. 'Callum and I have done enough damage to warrant what I did.'

'You were under the control of Mandragora,' the Doctor said. 'I broke him free of it, he broke you free.'

And Caitlin looked him in the eye, a tear rolling down her cheek. 'Madam Delphi never controlled me. Mandragora never controlled me, it didn't need to.'

'Then who told you to shoot Dara Morgan or whatever his name was?' Donna asked.

'His mind has been… slipping for days. He was beginning to remember things… he was a weak link. I had to eliminate him.'

'You had to what? Why? He might have just saved the human race! Is that what this has all been about?'

And Caitlin suddenly looked the Doctor straight in the eye. 'I don't know,' she said, a tear starting to well up. 'What have I become? What has working for this thing done to me? I just killed someone. Oh my God… I just shot him without thinking.'

'Bit late for tears, chum,' Donna said. 'Working with Mandragora, you've probably killed loads of people.'

'I know,' Caitlin said quietly. 'I was out of control, hungry for… for power. I wanted control over my life.'

'I control everything,' Madam Delphi pulsed back. 'Including your life!'

'No you don't, you stupid box of wires. I chose this life because I thought I wanted it. But you know what, I got it wrong.' Her fingers were flying over the keyboard now. 'I'm shutting down the wireless, putting up your firewalls.'

'That won't stop me.'

'No, But it'll isolate you for a bit.' Caitlin looked sadly at the Doctor. 'I've done my bit, Mr Time Lord. It's up to you now.' And she pushed her chair back and knocked into the Doctor. Apologising, she moved around him and walked over to Callum's dead body. 'We could've had the world,' she said as she knelt beside him.

The Doctor tried to make sense of Caitlin's words. Wireless. Firewalls. Pointless things, Madam Delphi was a far more powerful computer than that. He tapped the keyboard and a blast of purple Mandragora energy nearly took his fingers off. 'Now now, don't get grumpy.'

'I will still destroy you, Doctor. You will be—' And she fell silent.

Then he saw what Caitlin had really done. She'd talked nonsense, knowing that Madam Delphi would waste a few subroutines tracking down what she'd claimed to have done. Having found the firewalls and wireless untouched, the computer was now looking elsewhere. It would keep her silent and occupied for... well, not long, frankly.

But there was a calculation going on, he could see it on one of the screens, it was like a mini-virus itself, a self-replicating mathematical equation that was using up bytes with each passing second as, by trying to solve the equation, it actually multiplied it. The Doctor grinned. Caitlin was good at what she did, even if it would only take Madam Delphi another few seconds to counter it. He glanced towards Callum's body, expecting to see Caitlin.

The body was alone.

The Doctor felt his pockets. The revolver was still there. But something else wasn't.

'Donna,' he hissed. 'Donna, I want you to get down to the lobby. All those people will be confused, disorientated. Half of them might not even speak English for all we know. They need someone cool and rational to sort them out, explain things to them.'

'But as no one fitting that description is available,' Donna said, 'I'll have to do it.'

The Doctor grinned at her. 'Oh, Donna, you're the best there is. Now, off you go – no, not you, Wilf. You and Netty stay here.'

'Why can't they come with me?' Donna asked sharply.

'Family matters,' the Doctor said. 'Trust me, they'll both be downstairs safe and sound with me in a few minutes.'

'But…'

Wilf stepped up to the plate. 'Go on, Donna, don't argue with the man. When's he ever let you down?'

Donna went.

'Might not have been the best choice of words, Wilfred.'

'You ever let her down, Doctor?'

'Well…' the Doctor considered. 'No, actually, but it's been close once or twice.'

'Cos if I ever thought you'd let my little girl down, you'd have me to answer to.'

Their eyes met, across the room and, for the tiniest second, a fragment of eternity, the Doctor knew never, ever to let Donna Noble down.

'I won't,' he said. 'In fact, Wilf, I should say "we" won't, cos you're important right now. To Donna. To me. To the whole wide world. And most of all, to Henrietta Goodhart.' He suddenly stood up. 'Don't do it, Caitlin.'

Wilf realised the Irish girl was over by a wall, next to a junction box, holding a silver pen. With a blue tip that was glowing. 'What's she up to, then?'

'You don't know how to use it, Caitlin,' the Doctor said slowly. 'And Madam Delphi's gonna be up and running again in a second. She'll stop you.'

'Let her try,' Caitlin said. 'And you're right, I don't know how to use it, but I reckon if I push this, twist that and shove it all in there…'

'Cait, no!'

It was too late. As the sonic screwdriver suddenly shrieked with power, too much power, mishandled, used by untrained hands, Caitlin shoved it into the now-exposed junction box, and right into the fibre-optic cables that Johnnie Bates had died linking up only a few days earlier.

There was a flash of purple fire and Caitlin was gone, reduced to atoms along with a chunk of the wall, the cabling and the Doctor's sonic screwdriver.

'Right idea,' the Doctor said mournfully, 'but there had to be a better way.'

'That computer's gone off,' Wilf said.

The Doctor looked at the screens, and dived down to examine the server. 'Dead as a doornail,' he confirmed.

'We won?'

'Oh, not at all.' The Doctor looked at Wilf. 'I lied to Donna,' he confessed.

'I know,' Wilf said. 'But you made sure she was safe. Thank you.'

'Caitlin cut off the Mandragora energy from the computer. To all intents and purposes, Madam Delphi is gone. Erased. Destroyed.'

'But that Mandragora energy stuff, it's still there, isn't it?'

'Trapped.'

'Where?'

'In this room. And right now, it's looking for a new home. I reckon we've got about three minutes.'

'It won't choose me, that's why you kept me here. I heard what you said. I have a heart condition. I'm gonna die.'

'What?' The Doctor frowned, then remembered what he said earlier to Madam Delphi. 'Wilfred, I have no idea about the condition of your heart one way or another. You could have a couple more decades in you at least, for all I know. I was just saying that because – well, doesn't matter right now.' He glanced at the missing chunk of wall where Caitlin had been standing. 'Now, I doubt it can bring back the dead, so I'm hoping it goes for the easiest target, the path of least resistance.'

Wilf followed the Doctor's point of view to Netty, stood smiling serenely beside him.

'No…'

'It's the most likely vessel.'

Wilf was shaking with sadness. 'But it's my Netty. We were going to see the world, go on a cruise, do South America, Canada, the Indian Ocean. Doctor, she's my life. I never thought anyone could replace my wife, God rest her soul, but Netty Goodhart came along and showed me that there's more to living than sitting in a vegetable patch listening to Dusty Springfield. I can't lose her. I can't lose another lady from my life. I love her!'

'I know you do, and I'm really sorry to ask this of her, but I have to.'

'You can't ask her, she's… she's shut off right now. It's the illness, the dementia. She can't speak for herself.'

The Doctor reached into his pocket and took out a piece of paper.

Wilf looked at it.

My Darling Wilfred.

You told me once you trusted the Doctor with Donna's life. Now trust him with mine. I don't know what he's going to do, nor what state I'll be in when he does it, but if you trust him, that's good enough for me.

HG

'It's your special paper,' Wilf said. 'Shows me what I want to see. Donna told me about it, ages ago.'

The Doctor mouthed a silent 'oh, thank you very much, Donna', then produced his leather wallet with the real psychic paper in it. 'No, Wilfred, the letter's genuine. When we were at that burger place I explained to Netty what might be needed. Why she was a potential target and a potential—'

The Doctor broke off, and Wilf saw a momentary purple flash of fire shoot through his eyes. He then screwed them tight and opened them again. Brown. As always.

The Doctor blew air out of his cheeks. 'That wasn't fun, but it won't try me again.'

'No need,' said Henrietta Goodhart, quietly but with a familiar menace to her tone. 'I have a new home. A new body. One that can move, and talk, and feel.'

'Get out of my lady-friend,' Wilf snapped.

Netty just laughed. 'You poor pathetic deluded man. This is my vessel now. Mandragora lives. I shall rain down destruction upon this world, I shall have my revenge. This entire cosmos will fall into ruin and chaos and I shall feed off it for centuries. Beautiful chaos!'

Wilf took a step towards Netty, but the Doctor pulled him back, gave an almost imperceptible shake of his head.

'Wait.' The Doctor looked over at the burnt wall where Caitlin had died. Then at the computer, now useless and dead. At Callum Fitzhaugh's body, so consumed by rage and despair once upon a time, he had given succour to a universal blight that was about to destroy Earth, given a chance. And at Henrietta Goodhart's body, inhabited now by an alien power so great, it had survived since the Dark Times and was now ready to wreak a wave of annihilation across the known galaxies.

Unless he had got his calculations right.

Netty walked around the room, as if nothing were wrong with her, a strong, fit woman in her late sixties, who should have been yomping across the Yorkshire Dales or sunning herself on a Caribbean cruise, Wilfred Mott as her companion, at her side.

Instead, she coughed. She staggered.

Wilf went to help, but the Doctor yanked him back. 'I'm sorry, I can't begin to imagine how hard this is for you,' the Doctor told him, 'but you have to let it play out.'

Netty, or rather the alien life force currently inhabiting her mind and body, grinned at them. It was a grin neither of them liked much. It twisted Netty's face in a way that demonstrated absolutely that this was not Netty at all. 'Thank you, Doctor,' she gloated. 'You have given me a whole new lease of life. I always knew the computer was a means to an end, that one day the right host would come along. Having studied this ridiculous planet, I'd rather hoped it'd be a young, sexy, male body. Like a TV soap star or a sportsman. But hey, little old ladies will do for now. When this one is burned up, I'll move on to another.'

'Burned up?' Wilf looked at the Doctor, but the Time Lord's gaze was firmly fixed on Netty. Whether this was for a reason other than not being able to deal with Wilf's accusatory stare, Wilf had no idea.

'Oh, didn't your alien mate here tell you about that side of things? I wonder if he told Henrietta Goodhart when he made the deal with her. You see, Wilf – I may call you Wilf, mayn't I? Only Netty is terribly fond of you, and I think it makes things easier if we communicate casually. Mr Mott is terribly formal.' The rictus grin got wider. 'Anyway, the human body can only withstand Mandragora energy for a short time before it evaporates and I have to find a new repository. Ultimately, it will be the Doctor.'

'Will it? Oh joy.'

'You know it will.'

'But you need to weaken my defences first, of course. Batter me down, break my spirit. How're you going to do that, then?'

Netty laughed – it was a sound utterly devoid of warmth or genuine mirth. 'By destroying everyone you know.'

She suddenly looked unsteady on her feet, and reached out to Wilf for support. He was about to supply it when the Doctor bounded across the room, knocking Wilf's arm away.

'Oi!'

'Oh, don't you start,' the Doctor muttered. 'Let her stand on her own two feet.'

Netty was steady again. 'Starting with this old man with the bad heart.'

Wilf was about to speak – and then it dawned on him why the Doctor had made up the stuff about his heart. He'd wanted it to take Netty's body, not Wilf's.

Why?

'Once upon a time, Doctor, we saw this world as a threat, it had so much potential. We tried to stop it developing, hold back its early sciences. But look at it now! We were wrong, we should have encouraged it further. It has the ability to communicate. With one tiny computer virus, Mandragora can touch the world. There are almost seven billion people on Earth, Doctor. In a couple of years, two billion homes will have a personal computer within them, accessed on average by three people. Add to that infiltration into the workplace and it will take Mandragora less than an hour to effectively dominate the majority of people in this planet, to use human technology to spread Mandragora across the galaxy far more efficiently than I can do it alone. In twenty years, I could have humanity building farms on Mars. In a hundred years' time, we could colonise Alpha Centauri. A new Mandragoran Empire, combining Helix energy, human physicality and communications science. And then… then…'

'It's impressive, I'll grant you. Then what?'

'What does any species do? It flourishes, it dominates it… sort of… keeps going.'

'Oh, "sort of keeps going", that's very scientific.' The Doctor sat on the chair in front of the now useless Madam Delphi set-up. 'And? Tell me more of your plans. Wilfred here is desperate to know. So am I. And Donna, she's just outside the door – hello, Donna, come back in – I'm sure she wants to know, too.'

Donna showed herself. 'I thought I could be more help up here. All those weirdos, I ushered into the staff restaurant, told 'em I'd be back in a minute.'

'Umm, Donna,' the Doctor cautioned, 'what's to stop them running away?'

Donna held up a little silver key and waved it in front of his nose. 'Cos I'm brilliant and locked 'em in.' She grinned. 'Oh, but I sent the Carnes boys home.'

'Good, good. Mandragora here was just telling me how he/she/it is going to create a whole new empire. Like the Byzantine Empire, or, um, what was that other one? Greek? No… Oh, what was it?'

Donna opened her mouth to suggest 'Roman' but the Doctor stopped her.

'Now, now, Donna, let Mandragora work it out. Come on, you've got all that information at your fingertips, what's the empire I'm thinking of? Something to do with a Decline and a Fall, wasn't it?'

Netty/Mandragora paused. Then: 'Roman. The Roman Empire.'

'Oh yes, very good. How many billions of computers are there on Earth now? What was the market infiltration of the M-TEK, by the way?'

Netty/Mandragora frowned, and turned to Donna's granddad. 'Wilf? Help me…'

'Netty…?'

'No, Wilfred,' the Doctor said loudly, his voice suddenly like a gunshot. 'Sit down, leave Netty to work it out. Now!'

And Wilf settled next to Donna, on the floor.

'Where is Mandragora from?'

Netty/Mandragora smiled. 'A nebula, Doctor. We escaped the Dark Times and created a new home in the heart of beautiful chaos.'

'Of course you did. What was it called?'

'The… it was… I can't remember…' Netty/Mandragora staggered slightly. 'We can't remember…'

'Come on, focus,' the Doctor yelled suddenly, and he was up, circling Netty/Mandragora, firing questions as he walked around.

'Tell me the speed of light? How many years did the Carrionite-Eternals war rage? Where is the home world of the Judoon? What's the Twenty-Third Convention of the Shadow Proclamation? Who won the Bendrome/ Sendrome War? How many beans make five? Come on, come on…' he clicked his fingers impatiently. 'I mean, you can hardly take over the universe if you can't think for yourself, can you?'

'Give me a moment…' Netty/Mandragora spat.

'Give you a moment? Well, I could give you a moment, I s'pose, I mean, I'd give Henrietta Goodhart a moment or two happily, because she's not well, is she? Oh, didn't you realise? Hadn't you sussed that bit out?' And the Doctor roughly grabbed Netty's shoulders and swung her round so they were face to face, noses almost touching. 'You've taken on the body of a rather amazing lady, Mandragora, and you've locked yourself away in her mind, spreading out into her synapses and everything. Trouble is, the synapses are failing her. Each and every day the neurons and synapses in her cerebral cortex are atrophying. And you're speeding the process up in your hurry to acclimatise yourself and, sadly, you're already breaking up. I mean you can't think of words – that's a touch of paraphasia coming on. Unsteady on your feet? Well, I think that's apraxia. Temporal lobe, parietal lobe, decaying around you.'

'You… you did something… tricked… you tricked me…'

'Well… yes, I think I did. And the more you fight it, the more Mandragora energy you spend trying to repair those bits of brain, the more you're actually losing yourself, because this lady has Moderate Alzheimer's and that's not curable, even by you.'

'Then I shall, you know, change… move, swap bodies with… I shall…'

'Yes? What? What will you do? Go on, tell me.'

Donna joined in. 'Or you could tell us all about the stars, all those marvellous constellations, all the things that Netty knows about. Tell us where the Dog Star is? Or how to find the Big Dipper. What direction will I see Venus in at this time of year?'

Wilf grabbed Donna's arm. 'Stop it, Donna, you're confusing her.'

'That's the idea,' she told him. 'That's what the Doctor's doing this for, speeding up the confusion.'

'But it's Netty… you're hurting Netty!'

Wilf couldn't move. He knew that Donna and the Doctor knew what they were doing, but it didn't stop him wanting them to stop. Wanting to do anything other than have Netty used and abused in this way. But he didn't. Because, as he'd once read in a newspaper advice column, 'sometimes the greatest good can come out of the smallest pain.' Actually it had probably said 'life's full of hard knocks', but that was how he'd chosen to interpret it.

He just hated it.

For one teeny tiny second, he almost hated the Doctor and Donna for doing it so… easily.

And then he made a decision.

'When the stars begin to fall,' he began to sing quietly, 'Oh Lord! What a morning. Oh Lord! What a morning…' His voice cracked slightly, so he cleared his throat and began again. 'When the stars begin to fall, Oh Lord! What a morning. Oh Lord! What a morning. When the stars begin to fall…'

Gently, quietly, Netty's voice responded. 'Oh sinner, what will you do, when the stars begin to fall… Oh Lord! What a morning…'

Wilf reached out and took her hand, trying to hide his tears as he did so.

This time the Doctor didn't pull him away. Wilf started slow, stumbling dance steps with Netty, as the two of them sang quietly together the song that she so loved.

The Doctor eased Donna back. 'It's up to your granddad now,' he whispered.

'D'you remember where we first heard this song?' Wilf said to Netty as they danced. 'Who sang it? What was the name of the man who brought us dinner? Can you remember the car, all silver and shining? And was that the first time you'd ever been driven in a Rolls-Royce? And what I said at the end, as we drove through the streets, looking up at that clear, beautiful sky? And can you—'

'I… I can't… I can't remember… I am Mandr… Mandragora… I will rule the universe… somehow… I can't…'

'You are Henrietta Goodhart,' Wilf said gently. 'And you are ill, so terribly, terribly ill, and I'm so scared I'm gonna lose you and I don't want to lose you. Please stay.'

'Wilfred?'

The Doctor and Donna immediately perked up as Netty spoke his name.

'You're Wilfred… and I'm Netty… no, I'm the Mandragora Helix, and I… Oh Lord! What a morning…'

Wilf pulled her tightly to him, and hugged her more than he had ever hugged anyone since his beloved Eileen had passed away. 'Oh sinner, what will you do,' he sang back.

'My head… I don't understand… I can't remember anything…' Netty pushed him away. 'Why can't I remember? It's not fair… It's not fair! I can't remember anything… it's not fair!!'

Netty's head dropped backwards and she looked up at the ceiling, bringing both her hands up to point in the direction she was looking. The others watched as screaming purple, blue, red light roared from her body, utterly vaporising a space in the ceiling as the Mandragora energy erupted from Netty's human form and streaked up into the sky.

Then the noise and light cut off.

Mandragora was gone.

Netty's hands fell limply to her sides, and her head lolled forward.

Wilf went to catch her, but Netty just shook herself and looked up at him, a huge smile of recognition on her face.

'Wilfred?' She looked around the hotel penthouse, saw the perfect hole in the ceiling, then spotted the Doctor and Donna.

'Blimey O'Reilly,' she said. 'Have I been Sundowning again? Where on earth have I wandered off to this time?'

'You, Henrietta Goodhart,' the Doctor smiled, 'just saved planet Earth. You're brilliant.'

Donna nudged him. 'Yeah. And you're not so useless yourself, spaceman.'

A hundred miles. A thousand miles. A million miles. Moving almost at the speed of thought, the fractured, disembodied Mandragora Helix shot across the universe, screaming inside, its mind falling apart, trying to find its way home.

But where was home? Surely it was… No, it was… Where was home? Where was here?

Who am I? What am I? Why am I?

Who… what… where… how…

I think therefore I am…

I think therefore…

I think…

I…

What is 'I'…

Nothing…

'I' is nothing…

I…

I…

i…

…

..

.

In the canteen, Donna had taken charge, and she soon had everyone relaxed and sorted out, which was a relief for the Doctor – she was much better at this human touchy-feely stuff than him. More importantly right now, she could lie far more convincingly, tell them it'd all been part of a computer virus sent out by MorganTech and that they could go back home as soon as it was daylight.

The Doctor had made a couple of quick calls to people he knew in high places (or maybe low ones) and announced that someone would be arriving very soon to give everyone air tickets and first-class reservations to wherever they wanted to go.

'This is England,' the old American man had muttered. 'I always wanted to come to England. How on earth did I get here?'

The Doctor couldn't answer that one but instead fobbed him and his lovely wife off by saying he'd arranged for them to stay in a hotel (not this one, thank God) in the centre of town, and they had a seven-day pass to explore the city. 'Take the train out, go visit Bath, or Warwick or the Isle of Wight.'

'Or Hull,' Donna had added.

'Donna, why would they want to go to Hull? What's in Hull that they could possibly want to see?'

'I dunno,' she said. 'I've never been to Hull. But I always thought it sounded interesting.'

'Hull's lovely,' Wilf joined in. 'Went there for a long weekend once, to see a match. Went out on a boat.'

The Doctor gave in. 'All right,' he said to the Americans. 'Go to Hull, too. It has boats. Apparently.'

The elderly couple went off muttering about Hull, and the Doctor turned his attention to the students. Three guys and a girl.

'What happened to the Professor?' asked the girl.

The two guys at the back (oh, so a couple, Donna decided) nodded, but the other man looked downcast.

'He died, didn't he?'

The Doctor nodded. 'Italian man? Yes, I'm sorry.'

The students all stared at each other. 'I don't see any point in going back to Italy.'

'I do,' said the smaller guy at the back, looking at the other.

Ahhh, thought Donna.

'We should at least tie up loose ends out there,' the third guy said.

And the group wandered off, muttering together.

The Greek man was apologetic, saying he had no recollection of what he'd done, but guessed it hadn't been good. The Doctor explained it wasn't his fault and that he should go back to his family and forget about London. The man wandered off, muttering.

'Suppose he did something back in Greece? Suppose any of them did? Or all of them?' Donna said.

'I can't sort everything out, Donna.' He sighed. 'We can only hope that whatever has happened in their pasts, if anything, they can come to terms with it. And they're unlikely to actually remember.'

'You're thinking of your friend at Copernicus, aren't you?'

'One of them killed him. Broke his neck. Our Greek friend seems the most likely, but I'm not a policeman. And I can't prove anything.'

Donna pondered on the morality of it when her mobile phone bleeped. A text.

'Miss Oladini,' Donna waved her mobile at him. She read the text.

'Is she all right?' the Doctor asked.

'She's ecstatic. What did you do?'

'Dunno what you mean.'

'Doctor?'

'Well, perhaps while I was sorting things out with UNIT for that lot, I may possibly have mentioned how indebted we all were to her, too.'

'She says here,' Donna smiled, 'that she's had her visitor's status upgraded and can now come and go as she pleases. No more hiding. Oh, and she also says to tell you she has a cat called Dolly, and that you know what that means.'

The Doctor beamed. 'Good for them both.'

'Thought you didn't like cats much?'

'I always liked Dolly. And she deserves a good home.'

'Doctor? How many other people did Madam Delphi use and then chuck away?'

'Mankind were just tools to the Helix, tools to be used and abandoned.'

'Like Netty?'

The Doctor visibly winced.

'I'm sorry,' Donna said. 'That was below the belt.'

The Doctor looked at his friend. 'But true, and honest. I had to take the risk, Donna. Once, I might've done it with less conscience.'

'My God,' Donna said in mock horror. 'What have I done to you?'

The Doctor was serious. He took her hands in his. 'Made me a better person.'

Donna pulled her hands away, resorting. as always, to her standard jokes. 'Now then, don't touch what you can't afford, spaceman.'

They watched as Wilf and Netty started walking towards the main reception area. 'Let's get them back to your mum, eh?'

Donna nodded. 'You coming too, then? I mean, you know what she's like.'

The Doctor nodded. 'Yeah. An older version of her daughter.'

'Oi!' Donna laughed and linked arms with the Doctor. 'Come on, spaceman. You've stared down Sontarans, Pyroviles and the Fishmen of Kandalinga. I don't really think my mum's that scary.'

'You don't?'

'Nah. Unless it's Monday. Mondays, she gets one of her 'mares on. Is today Monday?'

'Today is indeed Monday.'

Donna held him a bit tighter. 'My turn to protect you then, eh?'

FRIDAY

A few days later, and mankind had, as it always did, coped and moved on. MorganTech had officially crashed and burned, it's CEO and executive staff declared bankrupt in absentia.

The M-TEKs had been recalled and destroyed and a warrant was sent out for the arrest of Dara Morgan, until the truth was established about his identity (or at least the fact that he *wasn't* Dara Morgan), at which point the whole MorganTech affair came under the jurisdiction of UNIT and vanished from public view. The people guarding the craters had woken up, completely baffled as to why they were there. They were arrested, but would no doubt all be freed once UNIT got involved.

The Noble family were heading to the RPS – Wilf was finally getting his dinner and the Naming Honour. Netty was with them, bustling around with Sylvia, getting ready, trying on hats with alarmingly larger feathers and laughing at silly little things along with Donna's mum.

Wilf and the Doctor had sensibly escaped to the back garden, drinking tea and discussing in hushed tones the Doctor's various adventures with 'the outer space robot people', with each tale usually ending in uproariously raucous laughter.

Donna wandered through the patio doors to hush them. 'You'll have Mum wondering what you're talking about, and then the game's up.'

'Not gonna tell her the truth, then?' The Doctor raised an eyebrow at both of them.

A quick look shot between grandfather and granddaughter, followed in unison by 'Are you mad?'

'She'd definitely kill you this time,' Donna said.

'After killing me for keeping secrets,' Wilf agreed.

The Doctor shrugged and changed the subject. 'So, tonight's little shindig. What time are you heading off?'

'*We* are heading off at seven,' Donna said.

The Doctor opened his mouth to protest, to say the last thing he wanted was another RPS dinner, another chance to be pooh-poohed by Doctor Crossland or get into a long, dreary, conversation with Ariadne Holt about finger-painting or her terrifying lack of sartorial elegance.

'Brilliant,' he said unenthusiastically. 'I may need to nip back to the TARDIS to, um, change my suit.'

Donna shook her head. 'You are staying right here, Sonny Jim.'

'Here?'

'Here.'

'No TARDIS? No suit?'

'No TARDIS, no suit, no emergency calls from Princess Leia suggesting you're her only hope.' Donna swept up the tea mugs. 'More tea?'

The Doctor nodded.

Sylvia emerged, phone to her ear. 'Really?' she was saying. 'Well it must've been stolen in all that kerfuffle with the lights and everything… Oh, right. Well *that's* a bit dodgy, hoping someone will steal your van for the insurance. Oh well, all right, I'll see you later. Bye, love.' She switched the phone off. 'Mr Webb's blue Transit got stolen – turns out he wanted it to go, left the keys in it and everything, so he could claim the insurance. Apparently it turned up, burned out, somewhere in the East End. I dunno, some people…' She had something else in her hands and she dropped it in front of Wilf.

It was the pile of pamphlets for the nursing homes, torn in half. 'I think Netty should move in here. With us.' She touched Wilf's cheek. 'With you.'

Wilf stood up and hugged his daughter.

'No,' said Netty from behind them all, looking magnificent in her latest hat. 'My mind is clearer now for the first time in ages. But I can't move in here, Sylvia.'

'Why not?' asked Wilf.

'Oh, you dear, sweet man,' Netty winked at him. 'You make me so happy, but I'm not a fool. It'd be good to stay with you while I'm compos mentis. But if… *when* I slide again, you two aren't equipped to deal with me. The strain, the pressure, it's not fair on you. On either of you.'

She scooped up the ripped pamphlets. 'If it's all right with you both, though, I could do with a lift to some of these, see if we can't find one we all like.'

Sylvia touched Netty's arm. 'That's a huge decision,' she said. 'Are you sure, because I wasn't just saying what I said to be nice. I think you should be here, part of the family.'

Netty looked at the Doctor. 'What do you think, Doctor?'

The Doctor looked at Sylvia, then Donna, then Wilf. Then finally back at Netty. 'I think, Henrietta Goodhart, that you are a wise, sensible, strong lady who knows her own mind better than we all realised and will do what's right.' He swiped the tea mugs from Donna's hands. 'And I'm not family, and I really want to bow out of this conversation gracefully, so I'll go and put the kettle on.'

He quickly walked back into the house, washed out the mugs and filled the kettle, looking out of the kitchen window at the group in the garden and smiled to himself.

'Chicken,' said a quiet voice in the doorway.

'It's your mum and granddad's life, Donna,' he said. 'Not anything to do with me. Families. *So* not my thing.'

Donna joined him by the sink, looking out of the window. 'She seems so… in control now. So…'

'Normal?'

'Well, I might not have used that word exactly, but yeah.'

'It won't last.'

Donna didn't look at him. 'Why not? Maybe storing all that Mandragora energy cleared her neural wotnots, sorted it all out.'

'It's at least second-stage Alzheimer's, Donna. That's decay,' he replied quietly. 'It doesn't get better, it mostly gets worse. There's no miracle cure, I'm afraid, no magic solution for Netty. Her mind is a bit like a car windscreen. In some respects, the Mandragora Helix was the carwash, cleaning it up for a while. But it won't be long before all the dirt and insects and dust and scratches come back. I'm sorry.'

'It's so wrong.'

'Yup, it is. But life is never as convenient as we'd like. There's a million ailments, illnesses and diseases in the universe. If I believed something as malign as Mandragora could erase just one of them, I'd let it. I'd have allowed it to remain, doing some good. But there's never any miracle cures for things like that. Life's not like that. But it shouldn't stop people looking because one day, they will find an answer.'

'And that'd mean you were wrong.'

The Doctor laughed. 'Yup. It happens sometimes. And sometimes I like it. I wish I could find a way to help her, but I can't.'

'What about Granddad?'

'He's a grown man. He's made a rational, adult decision to look after her for as long as he can. That makes Wilfred Mott a Very Good Man in my book.'

'Mine too.'

'Perhaps we should stay for a while, help Netty get settled in somewhere. You could spend some quality family time with your mum?'

Donna shook her head. 'We're fine at the moment. Another week, we'd be under each other's feet, fighting, yelling, sniping.'

Through the window, out in the garden, they watched Sylvia and Netty going through the brochures.

'Where's that tea, then, eh?' said Wilf from behind the Doctor and Donna.

'Granddad,' Donna said suddenly. 'Maybe I should

put you and Mum first. Perhaps I should stick around, help you out with Netty.' She looked at the Doctor. 'God knows, I'd miss you and all… that…' She pointed towards the sky. 'But maybe it's time to grow up a bit.'

Wilf hugged Donna. 'Sweetheart, what makes you happy?'

Without missing a beat, Donna looked at the Doctor.

'And you think I'd be happy knowing I was responsible for you giving all that up? Think Netty would?'

'But you and Mum, you need me…'

'Maybe, but we've managed OK for a while now. I'd rather know you were out there with the Doctor, doing for other planets and people what you did for Earth the other day.'

'And Netty?'

Wilf smiled sadly. 'She's ill, and eventually she'll go. So will I. And your Mum. And none of us will have seen and done all the marvellous and thrilling things you have. All them memories you'll have. Netty's illness could take her in five years or next Thursday. She could also walk in front of the Number 18 to Kew Gardens. I won't let her illness, or our sadness at you not being around, stop you living the life you've chosen. Out there. With him.'

The Doctor put an arm around Donna. 'I'll look after her.'

'Too right you will, mate, or there'll be trouble, remember?' Wilf switched the kettle off as it began to boil. 'Listen, I promise – me, your mum and Netty – we'll still be here next time you visit. I'm not letting Netty go anywhere, someone's gotta keep me on the straight and narrow.' Wilf began making the tea. 'You're a smashing lady, Donna Noble,' he said. 'And I'm proud to know you and love you.' He kissed her cheek. 'Now, go call a cab, I'm not risking your mum's driving after she's had a couple of sherries tonight.'

He passed a mug of tea to them both, and raised his in a toast.

'To family. And bonds that can never be broken.'

ONE DAY... (Reprise)

It was raining up on the hill, the steady patter-patter-patter hitting the vast golfing umbrella like bullets on tin. Truth be told, it was raining everywhere, but up on the hill, here in the allotment, that was the only place Wilfred Mott really cared about it raining right now.

He stared up at the stars, up at his star, still there, no longer heralding the destruction of Earth, humanity or anybody.

Not even Netty.

'How was she?' he said, hearing footsteps trudging through the soggy allotment behind him.

Sylvia sat beside him, gripping his thermos, testing to see how warm the tea inside was. 'I should've brought you up another one,' she said. 'We didn't go to see her. Donna's out with Susie Mair, and I couldn't face it.'

Wilf looked at his daughter. There was something…

She was holding an envelope out to him.

'Bit late for the post, darlin',' he said.

Sylvia didn't say anything, she just waggled the envelope at him.

Wilf took it. No stamp, hand delivered, addressed to MUM.

'Lukas Carnes delivered it this afternoon. He said she told him to do it six weeks after he last saw Donna, no matter what.'

'Did Donna see him?'

Sylvia shook her head. 'She was upstairs on the net. Didn't even hear the bell. Lukas lives in Reading now. I think the Doctor must've sorted it for them. Lukas thinks she's still…' Sylvia pointed to the stars. 'He thinks she's still out there, with him. No reason to spoil his dreams, is there?'

Wilf gave his daughter a hug. 'We'll get through all this, love.'

'We have to, don't we? For Donna, I mean.'

'And for the Doctor.'

'Who looks out for us now, Dad?' Sylvia suddenly said. 'I mean, I never liked the man, but even I know when I'm wrong. He saved the world, he made Donna happy. He kept us alive more than once. But if she's not with him, his link to this planet, what makes him come back here, to care about us?'

'Because he's good like that,' Wilf said. 'Because he's the Doctor and when we need him, he'll be there. It's what he does.'

'But what if he isn't? I mean, I felt safe before. I didn't know about Sontarans and Mandragora and Daleks. Not knowing kept us all safe. But now we all know the universe is so much bigger than us. Than you, or me. Or even Donna.'

Wilf looked up at the stars again, just in case that marvellous old TARDIS flew past.

Nothing.

'Well, there'll always be someone.'

He opened the letter.

Sylvia stood up. 'I'll go get you another thermos, OK. Back soon.' And Sylvia reached down to kiss his cheek, but instead gave him a massive, and frankly too tight, hug. 'I love you, Dad,' she said quietly.

Then she was gone.

Donna wasn't the only one the Doctor had changed, Wilf thought a little sadly and, at the same time, a little happily. Sylvia Noble was a more stable person, all told, these days. So what was in this letter that had made her so… touchy-feely tonight, then?

He reached into his bag and got out a little halogen torch he used to read his astrology books by when he was out at night.

He recognised the writing, of course.

Donna's.

His lovely, clever, brave, beautiful Donna's.

Dear Mum

You asked me what I do. What the Doctor and I do. And I lied. I'm sorry. I told you he was a fixer, that we nipped around the country and fixed things. That I was his PA. Not true. Well, of course it isn't and I'm not sure you believed me anyway, you're my old mum, you're sharper than that. Remember what Nanna Mott always said? You can't hide secrets, cos there's no such thing. Someone always knows — otherwise who told you the secret in the first place? So true.

Well, a couple of years ago, I was drifting. Job to job, place to place – thank God I took that job at H.C. Clements. Thank God I let you nag me into it (even if it wasn't actually the job you wanted me to do) – not that I told you that then of course, oh no. That would've let you off the hook too easily.

But I am glad you did, Mum. Cos that's how I met the most fantastic man (and no, not poor Lance. One day, promise, I'll tell you the true story of him).

I met the Doctor. He's an alien, Mum. But I think you guessed that. I'm not sure why you don't like him much, but I often wonder if it's cos he took me away, and I think there's part of you that can't accept that he's the one who really changed me. Made me happy. Made me a better person.

I'm sorry, that came out wrong, I'm not blaming you. You gave me the best life. Really you did. But he shows me there's more.

You asked how long I plan on staying with him. For Ever. Which, in his line of work, could mean anything. But I'm not coming home any time soon. I promise I'll visit more and write more cards. I'll try and phone more often, too. You wouldn't believe what he's done to my mobile – makes the rest of them look like tin cans and a bit of string.

No, we're not a 'couple' – there's nothing romantic

in him. He's my friend. He's my best friend. I hope I'm explaining this to you properly. I couldn't say it to your face, I had to write it down.

I was going to do it as a speech but then thought as you like letters, I'd actually write one. First time I've written a letter that didn't end 'yours faithfully' since Auntie Maureen's Christmas blouse. What was I, 14? And you know how that turned out – don't think I've written this much since then!

He looks after me, Mum. You have to trust him. I do. And I hope that if I trust him, you will too. Granddad does. He knows – and please don't yell at him, it was me who made him promise not to tell you what we do. Because you'd worry.

Oh Mum – you should see what I see. We've been to places, to worlds, to futures and pasts you could only dream about. I think half of them I dreamed up cos they can't be real. But they are. And everywhere we go, we make a difference. We put things right, we make people happier. That's what the Doctor is all about. He finds a way for the universe to make sense. And I love him for it. Because he's selfless, and I think that's rubbed off on me a bit but clearly not enough because I should've known how much you were hurting. I should've known that just coming home for Dad's anniversary wasn't enough.

You need me, but he needs me even more.

And that is awful because I love you, Mum, and not being able to be there for you is wrong, but I need you to understand the reason I'm not there more often.

I am going to keep travelling with the Doctor to other planets, other worlds, and meet aliens and stuff, good ones and a few bad ones, because I'm finally living my life. All these years, I waited for someone like him and I never realised it. But now I know I'm doing the right thing. I feel alive.

And he'll look after me as much as I look after him. Trust me when I say I'm safe and I'll always be safe. And if anything does happen to me (and it better not cos I'll come back and haunt his skinny little life for ever) I know he won't leave you wondering. He'll tell you no matter how hard that would be for him. Because he understands being alone and how wrong that is and I don't think my little spaceman would wish that on anyone.

I love you, Mum, and by the time you get this (assuming Lukas does what he's asked) I'll be long gone again. But that's the joy of being with the Doctor. I could be back before you know it. Six weeks might have gone for me, six minutes for you.

Take care of Granddad. And that lovely Netty – she's good for him, and I think you know that now. She's not trying to be a replacement for Nanna Eileen, she's an alternative. And it gives him something else to do other than sit in damp allotments all night.

I love you so much and I'll see you soon.

D
xxx

After reading it twice more, Wilf kissed the signature and carefully put the letter back in the envelope.

He thought about the Doctor, what Donna had said about loneliness. And remembered that sad – so, *so* sad – look on his face in the rain that night.

He had brought her home. He had faced them, just as Donna had known he would.

Sylvia had a point, too, though. Without Donna to bring him back here, what guarantee was there that he would save Earth next time?

It was too easy to just say 'Oh well, someone'll do it'. Maybe someone else had to stand up, and be ready to be counted.

So Wilf stood up and stared into the stars, feeling the rain beat against his face.

He saluted the night sky.

'Dunno if you're out there, Doctor, watching over us. But I reckon you are. Because I reckon that's what you do for everyone, on every world, everywhere. But I think we also need to learn to stand on our own two feet, too. Not take you for granted.'

He wiped rain from his eyes – at least, he decided to say it was rain. If anyone asked.

And Wilfred Mott glanced back down from the

allotment across West London below, lit up at night.

No aliens seemed to be invading, no supercomputers seemed to be destroying lives.

And he just thought about friendship.

'Come back soon, Doctor,' he muttered. 'Not just when we need you. Pop in for a cuppa one day.'

ACKNOWLEDGEMENTS

This book is only in your hands because Justin Richards and Steve Tribe (editors extraordinaire) worked so hard to get it there. I am very, very grateful to them. More than they realise.

Thanks are due to Russell T Davies, who put me on the right path with Donna and Wilf; to Lee Binding for his inspirational cover; to James North in the *Doctor Who* Art Department for his research; and the following people who, quite genuinely, kept me sane when I freaked out: John Ainsworth, Edward Russell, Ben Brown, Lindsey Alford, Brian Minchin, Darren Scott and most especially Joe Lidster.

Next in the Doctor Who *50th Anniversary Collection:*

THE SILENT STARS GO BY
DAN ABNETT

ISBN 978 1 849 90517 6

The Doctor Who *50th Anniversary Collection*
Eleven classic adventures
Eleven brilliant writers
One incredible Doctor

The winter festival is approaching for the hardy colony of
Morphans, but no one is in the mood to celebrate. They're
trying to build a new life on a cold new world, but each year
gets harder and harder. It's almost as if some dark force is
working against them. Then three mysterious travelers arrive
out of the midwinter night, one of them claiming to be a
doctor. Are they bringing the gift of salvation or doom? And
what else might be lurking out there, about to wake up?

An adventure featuring the Eleventh Doctor, as played by Matt Smith,
and his companions Amy and Rory.

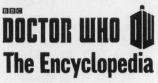

DOCTOR WHO
The Encyclopedia

Gary Russell

Available for iPad
An unforgettable tour of space and time!

The ultimate series companion and episode guide, covering seven thrilling years of *Doctor Who*. Download everything that has happened, un-happened and happened again in the worlds of the Ninth, Tenth and Eleventh Doctors.

◊

Explore and search over three thousand entries by episode, character, place or object and see the connections that link them together

◊

Open interactive 'portals' for the Doctor, Amy, Rory, River and other major characters

◊

Build an A-Z of your favourites, explore galleries of imagery, and preview and buy must-have episodes